The Plutonium Kid
and other stories

Stanley Heidrich

The Plutonium Kid

and other stories

For Delana

Published by Swordmyth Books

ISBN 978-0-615-60451-0

Contents

Beyond Innocence

"Here in Hell," said the loathsome Luther, introducing me to the place he assumed would be my residence for all eternity, "there is no need for pride." And he guided me across flat parched ground and through an abbeviated tunnel. We climbed a barren hillock to where a mustard-like sun shone through a stand of leafless trees.

Luther had reached his position of influence in Hell while exploring the limits of his cynical misanthropy. A young man when he arrived—stabbed multiple times by a jealous mistress—he had cultivated the appearance of an old man, and the juxtaposition of youth and decrepitude was intimidating. Although his skin was pale like that of an apparition, his wispy hair stayed dark as tar, with his glittering eyes concealed behind opaque round lenses in a steel frame. A well-worn tuxedo flapping around his gauntness gave him a disconcertingly fragile appearance and he never removed the black skullcap on his head, but his movements had the deceptively smooth grace of a young athlete.

But how does one describe his face? Even catching a glimpse of it in one's peripheral vision made the heart shudder. His eyes behind the glasses looked like small black orbs. His nose was comprised of two tilted flat planes with a horizontal base like an equilateral triangle into which a pair of nostril holes had been punched. His cheeks were sunken hollows and belly-white like the rest of him. And his mouth was the real horror. It could hardly be called a mouth, since it served that function with none of the shapeliness we associate with human mouths. Luther's was just a large orifice in his face. It had no lips or teeth, being hard and thin like an insect's. Even worse, it never completely closed, and on the inside there was no healthy pink visible, only a cavernous grey space. The effect was appalling but hypnotic. One shrank from him but one couldn't walk away.

I don't need to describe myself. Who I was and who I am becomes clear as this story is told. It suffices to say that when I found myself in Hell I was no older than Luther when he arrived.

Luther brought me to a halt. He turned his horrid black marble eyes on me.

"Auto accident, wasn't it? You were driving drunk?"

"It's possible."

"It's certain. You stank of alcohol when you arrived."

"That must be why I don't remember my transit over the river Styx."

"Do the religious charlatans still peddle that myth?" Luther tilted his face toward the ersatz sky, a vague void with no discernible color. "There must have been a woman, of course. Some enchantress. She abandoned you and it was unbearable to live without her? Is that fair to say?"

"Not quite that romantic," I said. "Hamlet more than Romeo."

"An intellectual? Then I have the perfect mate for you." With these words he guided me to meet Mabel, a corpulent slattern with the grace of a walrus.

"No, thanks," I said, but he waved off my objection and strolled on.

I cast my gaze about my surroundings with the idea of exploring, but held back. Absurdly, I was concerned that I might get lost. Mabel grasped my wrist and pulled me down.

"Hot day, ain't it?" She gave a coarse giggle.

I pulled free and turned my back on her.

"If you try, you might even like me a little. Here." She rested two overly-plump hands on my shoulders. "You relax a bit, honey, and maybe you can sleep." Once again she gave that awful giggle that made her whole bulk quiver. "Whadyathink? You might wake up later and find out it's all a bad dream and you're back in the saddle with your sleeping beauty cutey."

That hope didn't get far in my mind. An intellectual has some skills in that respect. Besides, Mabel's chubby hands were active and I accepted the distraction.

I bedded with Mabel for three weeks while waiting for Luther's return and discovered that I wasn't so far above her fat lasciviousness and imbecilic jokes as my initial contempt had led me to suppose. Poor dear Mabel, with her rolls of flab she looked like a misshapen putty doll. Her face was a caricature of self-loathing and her voice shrill with self-mockery. By the third week she had unlocked a small measure of affection in my heart, and when Luther came back and led me away I hesitated. Glancing back at her lolling on the embankment, I felt the urge to kiss her goodbye.

"Are you so emotionally naïve you don't recognize pity when you feel it?" Luther asked with droll humor. Mabel must have heard, but she didn't seem to take offense.

Fifty paces on, having passed back through the tunnel, my heart breathed free again. Love, I reminded myself, doesn't stifle the lover or receiver. Emotional quagmires are many and varied, but love isn't one of them. It wasn't love I felt for Mabel, although in time I did return to her.

All the refined emotions evaporated in that godless oven. I saw a child savagely beaten by a passing stranger whom the child had inadvertently offended, but no cry of "brute!" sprang from anyone's lips. Even the child's mother paid no heed. She noticed but didn't interrupt the vulgar tryst that occupied her. When finished, she untangled herself and sauntered to the battered child. After a short look she twisted her face in disgust and returned to the old bugger of her affections. But should one call them affections? When she bent over the child's body, I strained to see even a hint of compassion or even melancholy at the doom that engulfed them all. I saw nothing. She simply no longer cared.

Not that I had much experience with the nuances of emotion. Linguistics had taught me how people think and talk, but had failed to educate me in how people feel. I thought of emotions as incidental by-products of the more meaningful human interactions. That's why I had been swept into a whirlpool of psychic turmoil when I fell in love with Lily. Neither of us knew what to do with the passion, except of course the obvious.

But it didn't stop there. It never does. Passions want to graduate into emotions, and emotions want to be expressed as words, and then words demand that reality be shaped to their description. Sometimes reality doesn't object to being fashioned by words, but other times it

3

does. Ours was such a case, and the reason was as old as the hills: Lily already had a husband.

Her conjugal status seemed a trivial obstacle in the way of our destiny and within weeks she left her husband. Without a doubt we weren't the first lovers believing we belonged together, without a doubt not the last. And no doubt we weren't the first to discover that destiny is a fraud that guarantees nothing. One year to the day after leaving her husband, she went back to him.

In the quarter century I lived as a mortal on earth, I never came across a landscape as bleak as that of Hell. That I might have endured with some adjustment. What weighed most on my heart as the months passed was the spiritual desolation there. According to Christian mythology, Hell collects souls, but a more soulless environment couldn't be imagined. Like the landscape, it was utterly flat in spirit, and little by little the emptiness eroded my own spirit. Had I ended up there before I knew Lily, I might not have noticed or cared. Before her I hadn't paid much attention to my spirit. Now its waning tormented me.

A large part of the problem was that Hell allowed nothing for the soul to celebrate. A glaring white sun rose every morning at the same point on the knife-edge horizon. Late every afternoon came the same infernal orange sunset, with the sun descending unaltered in size until it vanished at the same point without fail.

A warm rain fell midday for fifteen minutes. Perhaps I was losing my senses, but it occurred to me after a while that if by some demented technique I could document the pattern of raindrops on the parched ground, I would likely find no variance there from day to day or week to week.

Carnal arrangements were random but redundant. It was of little consequence that new faces appeared all the time. The new ones were close reproductions of arrivals a month or two, a year or two, earlier. Like everything else in Hell, sexual acts quickly became repetitive and were just as pointless. They didn't involve reproduction or love or even the small pleasure of amusement. They provided numbing physical release from the boredom, nothing more.

This soulless landscape spread. Hell grew constantly. Every hour I found a new crack in the ground and watched as it filled in with the anguishes of newcomers. Luther explained this to me with patient condescension. In the beginning, he said, Hell had been an infinitesimal point in the vastness of space. As it populated with lost souls, the point expanded into a plot of hard ground. By incorporating the scars on souls that Hell took in, the terrain now stretched toward infinity.

"Surely that defies logic," I countered. "If the universe is infinite and Hell becomes infinite, then two infinities would occupy the same space."

"After a while longer you won't care," Luther said, "so I'll give you the short version. Think of Hell as an alternate universe, with a door open between the two worlds. The threshold of that door is the human tolerance for misery. But between the two worlds there is a single continuum of matter and energy. Whatever we add here to Hell, we borrow from your material world. The material universe you think of as an infinity hasn't stopped shrinking since the first point in Hell was anchored."

He aimed a long pale finger at me.

"That," he said, with a harsh cackle from his hollow grey mouth, "is why you should adjust to your stay as painlessly as possible and without any regrets. Because in the not too distant future, there will be nothing, nothing at all anywhere, except here. Hell will triumph in the end because misery will never stop dying to get in." He winked as if reading my thoughts. "But you needn't be troubled by that certainty. By then, you'll care no more than Mabel does."

I had grown at ease with Luther despite his horrible insect face, because of his acute intellect and his indulgence with my curiosity. At times, though, I found his pronouncements disturbing. I had an objection to this particular one but he shrugged it off.

"Concern comes with looking forward," he said, "and boredom with looking back. You need neither in Hell. You pass the time without paying attention to it. You don't hope or regret. You don't suffer. You merely pass the time…"

I remained logical, as had been my lifelong habit. I pondered and reasoned, weighing various possibilities, filing them away or rejecting

5

them. I intended to understand my circumstances. It seemed to me that I couldn't have been cast adrift without some purpose. I had to discover what that purpose was. I wondered about the role God played but reached no certain conclusion, so I finally asked Luther.

"Now you have disappointed me," he responded.

Assuming that I'd committed some cardinal anti-sin by mentioning His name, I stammered an apology. It got me a sneer of disdain from Luther.

"Pah! It's not that. But I hadn't expected you to capitulate to that question for another year or more. I overestimated your intelligence."

This angered me and I raised my voice.

"Well, then, what about Him? He must know what's going on here! Why doesn't He put a stop to this farce? It must be within His power!"

"You already suspect the truth," Luther sighed. "Or you wouldn't ask."

"God!" I shouted. "What about God?"

Luther's mouth contorted oddly. "There's an ocean of rage beneath your intellectual façade, isn't there? All right, then. Tell me, have you caught the briefest glimpse of the Devil anywhere in Hell?"

After a moment of confusion I shook my head. I experienced a peculiar prickling of fear, the sort of fear that a thinking man dreads as much as being categorically wrong.

"And what does that tell you?"

"There is no Devil?" I asked weakly.

"Assuredly not."

"You want me to believe that God is a fiction, too?"

Luther nodded.

"What about Heaven?"

"There's no Heaven, either. There's only us…" With a finger he traced the sign of infinity in the air. "And them," he said, pointing emphatically downward.

"But what about ones that weren't damned? Where did they go?"

"They die and their bodies rot in the earth," Luther said as if speaking to an idiot. "The atoms of their mortal remains are dispersed into the cosmos, if you prefer a more poetic explanation."

"Then why am I here? Why is Mabel here? Why are you here?"

"Not for punishment, if that's what you're getting at. I like to explain it this way: think of the self as a puzzle of interlocked pieces. If it easily disassembles when death happens, it disperses into the material universe. If it can't, if during mortal existence the self has become too locked up with pain and fear, then it doesn't disintegrate like it should. It winds up here."

And that's what happened to me?—I wanted to ask, but I couldn't bring myself to voice the words. For months I turned these revelations over in my mind, growing increasingly furious at myself for my earthly foolishness. How could I have tied my soul up in such terrible knots that even ordinary death was denied me? I walked about cursing myself but I didn't yet surrender to despair. Such is the stubborn stamina of the intellectual.

Or so I thought. Then one day I sought out Luther and forgot where I was going. I struggled to recall my destination in the way one shrugs off a heavy drowsiness by shaking one's head. At last I remembered my intention, but I knew the end condition was growing near for me. When I located Luther I admitted my experience to him.

"You've held out longer than I expected," he said, as if it were a consolation prize.

"Damn it, Luther! I have to know how you do it! How is it that you avoid…" Unwilling to voice the words that terrified me, I gestured to express them.

Luther removed his dark glasses. His small eyes glittered like anthracite marbles.

"I take interest in ones like you," he said. "The proud and vain who thought their egos were more important than anything else. The ones who didn't value life itself."

"But you've seen a hundred like me."

"You flatter yourself like every other elitist. Tens of thousands exactly like you."

"Then of what possible interest is one more?"

It was desperation. I clutched at straws as I drowned. I was losing the ability to organize my thoughts. Hell was the dead-end of all intellectuals, the cul-de-sac where reasoning sank into the swamp of lethargy and joined the ranks of brutes and buggers.

Luther preened at my expense.

7

"Not much at all," he replied. "But that's the point. With every new one I make exciting new differentiations. I fine-tune my perceptions. You'd be astonished how exact a judge of character I've become."

"Then why," I groaned, "can't I keep from losing my mind the same way?"

In answer he reached out, seized a lock of my hair, and yanked with such force he tore it from my scalp. I howled with pain and swore with every epithet I knew, while pressing my palms on the bleeding rawness at my temple.

Luther watched me with smug satisfaction.

"Am I concerned you might strike me?" he mused. "No. You won't do it. That is how well I can predict you. I could toy with you all afternoon."

"You're sadistic!" I shouted. "That's what keeps you going! You have a captive audience of suffering masochists to torture! But don't kid yourself that you're superior! You ended up here, too!"

"I *chose* to come here, you fool!" he chortled, and boxed my ears.

It was then that I realized arguing with Luther was futile. It was like throwing oneself against a stone wall. What made it so humiliating was that my greatest fear was that Luther would walk away and leave me alone in my defeat. Beaten, I was at his mercy.

"You intellectuals!" he crowed. "How many reasons can you give yourself for not punching your puny fists at me? I've hurt you, you should hit back. True? But you don't. All of your life you smothered your emotions so that you could think. Why? Because of nameless fear in your soul, fear that now ties your hands. The dreaded fear of losing your control! Isn't that what all the thinking is about, eh?"

He parked his pale fists on his hips and leaned toward me with his insect head cocked.

"But look what that thinking did to your emotions. You're still a child! Lust and rage are all you know! And you're afraid of those, so you smother them with even more thinking."

He did a spry little dance, clicked his heels, and spread his arms dramatically.

8

"Lo! Along comes the enchantress! She glides in on your dark side, in between the shadowy myths and the baser instincts. The grip of your logic can get no purchase—you fall in love! And then there's the torrent of emotions. You're drowning in the flood and your intellect fights tooth and nail to keep your head!"

He snickered derisively.

"What I find most curious is that none of you change. Here you are in Hell. Here you could vent your so primitive emotions. Impulses to violence, lust and rage, they have no consequences here. No police, no juries, no worries about reputation or social status. Here you are in Hell and you elevate your stupid logic even higher! You expect to understand it! As if by understanding you'll come to some gentleman's agreement with your unexpressed self! And then you come to me for consolation when it doesn't work. You bore me now!" He stepped back, his face flushed with contempt. "Go away, you stupid wretch!"

He stalked off as I had feared he would. I knew that when our paths crossed again he would only nod, with a sardonic grin to imply the secrets he had plucked from me. He would greet me with the same sneering disinterest he greeted Mabel and the others.

I paced aimlessly in a fever that stayed me from sinking into the common lassitude. Those in my path I elbowed aside. The trysts I stumbled into earned a vicious kick rather than a muttered apology. Madness appealed to me, but I knew it would be pointless. In that wasteland, madness could be only a temporary refuge.

At last self-pity brought me down. I howled like a baby at his circumcision, but was offered not a word of kindness from anyone. A morning came when I awoke curled up next to Mabel's shallow-breathing bulk, and that morning I determined to escape.

I found it. That must have dealt Luther a rude jolt. It must have tormented his mind through a thousand of my approximate replicas. The solution was so obvious that I wondered how many others had found it and already employed it.

The fabric of Hell, you see, is scars. Scratching out a circle on the parched ground, equal in circumference to the widest part of my body, I labeled every square millimeter of that space for one of countless wounds my heart had suffered during life in the material world.

Then I enlisted the aid of Mabel, who positioned herself above me with her obese legs bent over my shoulders. Quickly I yanked each scar from the ground. As the circle underneath me softened into a bloody mass of anguish and pain, I shrieked for Mabel to drop. She plopped with an awful weight onto my shoulders and I sank into the firmament. My mind buzzed with dizzying pain, I smelled the caustic odor of Mabel's pudendum, and I screamed out of Hell as a newborn squeezes from the womb.

*

Like a tendril of fog I wandered the sidewalks of San Francisco. Its multitude of inhabitants, protected by familiar blinders, moved around me with jerky gaits. Men served themselves up to women with desire while women served themselves up to the men for adoration, and I knew that somewhere among them was the woman who now understood it wasn't that easy—to desire and adore, to be desired and adored, to slip into such facile relationships in the panorama of history's delusions. Lily's sudden laugh and dancing eyes, her swift wetness, her dark hard nipples, these were all that were real to me in the overstuffed world I had once striven to explain with science.

Had I but a yellow and black Western Union telegram to mail my love on! My eyes no longer saw clearly, my voice was hoarse, my hands clumsy. I was weightless and weak. Hell had laid waste to me, Hell had stolen my substance. I was buffeted by every zephyr and driven headlong by every strong wind.

Eventually I began to listen in a different manner. Not seeing the endless parade of faces with my eyes, not hearing the babbling voices with my ears, but instead feeling them about me. I felt the warm gravitation of their bodies coming close, passing by, and growing distant again. I felt their waxing and waning coronas, the electronic music of their brainwaves. Through the massive earth with its brute gravity, through the stellar echoes, I began to distinguish the delicate mist of human interaction. I could feel the tremulous touches of new lovers, sense the soft explosions of their shared pleasures. I could feel the caresses of mothers with infants, sense their synchronized heartbeats.

The crowded buildings and street traffic faded into background and then disappeared altogether, until what remained was an ever-ascending crescendo of pure humanity, the glittering and spangled energy mist of a million human beings being human in ever-shifting relationships.

She was among them somewhere. Often I caught her scent in a crosstown breeze, a teasing hint that swept quickly by me before I could pinpoint its origin. Finally on a wet afternoon with winds roaring in from the beach in furious gusts, I realized why that was. Lily was evading me.

I bore on relentlessly. To find her became the sole task in my afterlife. I forgot how to think, how to observe and reason, except insofar as those skills enabled me to distinguish her scent and her patterns of travel, her haunts and paths, her tactics of elusion. At last I could predict even the tactical zig-zags she changed day to day. Then I began to gain on her.

One cold January morning I caught up to her. She was walking as I had seen her in a hundred dreams, walking fast with her arms folded under her breasts, hugging herself tightly. She hurried her pace as she felt my presence close on her heels, but I was the wind itself. Lottery tickets and candy wrappers fluttered madly in the wake of my disembodied spirit. I hurtled down the pastel avenues, past the look-alike stucco bungalows, and ahead of me her rapid steps lost their rhythm.

There was a short hesitation in her progress, then a few more hurried steps. She halted again and this time turned. I approached so closely that I could feel her warm breaths as the tempo of her respiration returned to normal.

She spoke my name in a low voice and the single word so overwhelmed me that for a minute we faced each other silently, as if the eternal struggle of humanity had finally created perfection and nothing could possibly be added to it.

Then a dog barked. Lily glanced in that direction and giggled in her self-deprecating way.

"Oh!" she said, cutting short the laugh and looking aside. "I knew this would happen, but I never figured out what I was going to say. Now I feel kind of dumb, just standing here."

11

So I told her of Hell, I told her of death and resurrection, and she listened, watching me with the same attentiveness as when we were lovers.

"Lily, we can start over," I told her when I had finished. "We won't fight anymore. We can be happy again, I swear we can."

"I wanted that for so long," she said wistfully. "I cried myself to sleep after all of our fights." She averted her face and gave a sigh, a melancholy exhalation. "My husband isn't the most exciting man in the world, but he's a lot easier to get along with." Then she faced me squarely. "I want to forget all that, all right? I want to remember you the way you were in the beginning."

"Lily, I can be like that again!"

Her eyes searched my face for a few moments. Then she shook her head.

"No," she said. "We lost our chance. We were innocent then. What we did was crazy, but we were so much in love we couldn't help it. If we tried to do it again it wouldn't be crazy. It wouldn't work."

"Don't you see?" I cried. "That's why it would work!"

"No! You can't go back to another time!"

Her eyes flashed with terrible fear and then stared dully at me, seeing nothing, perhaps, while thinking she saw everything. Maybe she had never known any love but that of life's futility, and the spell of that evil magic had nipped in the bud any hope for genuine love. She was damned as I had been, and more afraid to dream than to be unfulfilled, because dreams could become nightmares. Tears welled in my vacant eyes. For her, yes, for Lily, but for all my friends in San Francisco, in the world, in the vast array of stars and planets, everyone who had wished at one time or another for a swift vivisection of hope from the human condition.

I watched her swing away from me, running forever into the sanctuary of apathy. She leaned into the chilling winter winds while they, accessories to the criminal negligence, circled around and about her passing form.

Now I can recognize the curse that falls on my people. Not the heartlessness of institutions, not the machinations of men like Luther, not the mesmery of consumerism, but our ineluctable mortality is what separates us from the laughing stars. The gloom through which we miserably peer is a protective shield, and we cannot penetrate it often because we are consumed with fear.

The nuclear families that birth us and the schools that socialize us, the factories that grind us, the networks that entertain us, the leaders who lie lies until we are weary of asking for the truth, these are but makeshift props on a stage where we reveal our humanity in one two three acts of self-defense.

But free people need not defend themselves. I escaped my mortality and that is my freedom. Not that I can walk fearlessly among men and their machines, but that I have no need to know a thing, to learn a thing, to be a thing, no ideology, no expectation of the future, no struggle against a bogeyman called Fate with a chimera called Free Will.

Yet I do survive. I can be seen, I can be heard, and I cannot be killed. One might even say I have reached godhood. Slowly, slowly, I forget what it was like to be afraid to die. I forget my childhood, and the sensation then of snowflakes melting on my nose, and the sounds of thunder barking at the heels of lightning. I forget how I fell in love and how I gave pain.

Into the shabby hotels and bars of dismal night stream confessing men and weeping girls. A bus trundles through the late hour, and there come more, more, all of them damaged, all of them damned. I immerse myself in their bleak reality and they surround me, weary with their anguish as night unwinds into another tarnished dawn. Isn't it godhood to be able to cherish each one of them without judgment?

And I, this cluster of sparkling neurons and electromagnetic waves, will go on for an eternity. That isn't such a dreadful prospect. Time is a measure of sorrow and fear and despair. Having been emptied of them, time has vanished for me and despite my companions I am alone. Sometimes late at night the house is quiet and I stare into the fire and wish Lily were with me. But that also will cease. Then I will become the galaxian Methusaleh, having forgotten even that time before my innocence was lost, the time I can never go back to. Though I have longed for it dearly.

How Saber Got His Name

"Watch out for the wolfthing," his pappy had advised him.

A spectacular harvest moon was rising like a gold piece above the Drecker's barn, silhouetting junipers on the ridge and laying a shadow from the horsechestnut tree on which was nailed the plank with the words 'No Shooting' in faded white paint. Below that ridge was the hollow where blackberries grew, and that was where the wolfthing lurked. Never did Saber climb the ridge after darkness had fallen.

And if he happened to be coming home late from the Drecker house when dusk had brought out the bats and the fireflies, he went swiftly while casting glances from side to side and behind him, because his youthful skepticism dissolved in the darkness.

This particular evening, he galloped down the lane and stretched into full stride past the watering trough, because the sumac thicket was most tangled up there, and he was carrying the bag of salt that old man Drecker had picked up for them in town. Folktale claimed that the wolfthing settled for salt when it couldn't get warm flesh. Never-you-mind that sounded more like a vampire, huffed Sam Drecker, when Saber quarrelled the point. Never-you-mind, 'cause the one'll get you into the promised land and the other t' eternal twilight, if'n you stand on a principle about it, and you don't want neither.

"Watch yourself out for that wolfthing," his pappy had warned him as he shot off the porch heading to Dreckers' for the salt, and he was full tilt on his return run when he saw the shadows move.

Directly behind the horse watering trough, which was in disuse and overrun with thistle and milkweed, was the dark shape of a young woman. Saber slowed, agilely running sideways for a few strides, staring. He couldn't make out her features because she had her back to the moon. Then she moved soundlessly as if coming around the trough after him, and with a shout Saber lit out for home with blood pounding in his ears.

He never told his pappy about seeing the wolfthing. A ten-year old boy must keep some secrets.

"I never even told Grandpa," Saber said, sharing the story with Felicity when they fell in love.

"Because he was senile?" she asked.

Saber flushed. It embarrassed him to talk about growing up in Wyoming backwoods. Because, in the telling the rural past emerged as somewhat superior, instead of docilely shrinking behind his up-and-coming present. He couldn't reconcile the conflict there, so he typically avoided the subject of his upbringing.

"I don't mind where you grew up," Felicity told him, snuggling closer. "You don't have to be ashamed anymore."

And certainly he didn't. With a well-deserved scholarship to state university, he had ascended into the modern era. Ike was President, and Saber, smart as a whip, stood ready to help America conquer the world through big business. All he retained of his past was the name he had earned.

"Yay-hey, Say!" Grandpa would call, and Saber would shimmy down the cottonwood tree like a cat in flight from a clawing owl, because it meant Grandpa had entered a streak of lucidity. When that happened, he would lay down tales from his glorious collection of a hundred-forty years like pinouchle trump cards.

"Heck," Felicity went on, "I dated Denver boys whose grandaddies couldn't tell the difference between a Packard and a Plymouth. So tell me how you got the name, okay?"

How it happened was that one July afternoon his grandpa had stopped the mumblypeg grimacing of his toothless jaws and jumped out of the porch swing and named him on the spot. A hundred-forty is a powerful lot of years, the way Saber's pappy explained it: too much of what made you what you are and too big a life to keep it all in order. Which was supposedly why he didn't even measure time in days or weeks anymore. Why it was that when he did sometimes wander out of the swamp of senility, he remembered events only from whatever the current season was. In winter he'd cuss about it being so cold back in '89 that they left the icebox open to warm up the house, or if it was autumn he'd tell how back in Tennessee the leaves fell so thick you couldn't rake them but for getting the rake snagged on the treetops. And that sweltering mid-afternoon in July his only grandchild was hewing down a horde of attacking Huns with the parade sword that hadn't belonged to anybody and never came from anywhere when the hundred-forty year old man leaped out of the porch swing and yelped the name, and it stuck. In the porch post on which the suet birdfeeder hung.

"I would have guessed a different reason," Felicity giggled.

Taking a Chesterfield from the crumpled pack, she lit it and leaned to the window. With the shade lifted a few inches, Main Street sunlight shot into the hotel room like the projection beam at the drive-in, where her hands serviced him discreetly in her father's Buick Roadster.

"You mean this?" he asked, pulling her pale hand beneath the sheet.

Her breath caught with sudden desire. "Oh, stab me again, sweetie! Stab me all the way to the hilt!"

The shade dropped. The stream of sunlight vanished with the disembodied request to return the speakers to their stands before driving away. The hotel room went to dusky shadows.

*

On Christmas Eve, under the bewitching spell of Nat King Cole, Saber proposed to Felicity. Marrying in the spring, they fled the church steps under a shower of rice thrown by their modern friends. They bought and moved into a one-story bungalow in a post-war development in Denver.

Back home, his grandpa's episodes of senility lengthened until the seasonal gears worked fitfully even when engaged, and it was agreed by all except the old man himself that he should come to the city and stay with Saber and Felicity. This decision provoked him into defiant lucidity and he stayed where he was. The following November he lapsed into aphasic stupor, and was packed onto a Burlington Northern passenger train headed for Denver. He died with a phlegmy rattle in his throat as the train pulled into the station.

Saber's new boss, a Mr. Fielding, recommended a funeral parlor. With his pappy preferring to say his few words when interring the body back home in Wyoming, the service in Denver became Saber's responsibility. The event fell short of what Saber imagined a funeral should be. Insofar as it did, however, Saber reminded himself that if his grandpappy had been the sentimental type he wouldn't have so blithely outlived his contemporaries.

The modestly priced casket was shut by the undertaker's assistant, a chubby youth whose sharply creased slacks were either too short cut or too outgrown, and the syrupy organ stopped abruptly as the few mourners filed outside. Felicity had her black-gloved hands on her big belly in a way that Saber found rather funny, as if she didn't trust that the huge curvature was really part of her.

She leaned close to whisper to him, and off-balance nearly stumbled.

"Didn't he look real?" she asked enthusiastically.

"No," Saber grunted. "But you never saw him when he was alive."

"Well," she said, "I still think he looked awfully real. And you still haven't answered me, anyway."

Saber inhaled deeply the crisp November air. It was Saturday morning, and children tested sleds on the thin overnight snow.

"What's that, darling?"

"Was he really a hundred-forty back then? Because I was thinking about it. If he was that age when you were a boy, he'd be closer to a hundred-sixty now. And I'm positively sure nobody has ever lived that long."

Saber looked at her curiously.

"Then I guess he was still a hundred-forty when he died," he said.

Blackbourne the undertaker, a ruddy-complected man whose robust health belied his profession, joined them on the steps.

"I appreciated your eulogy," Saber told him.

Saber had known few factual details of his grandpa's life, so he had let Blackbourne weave into the narrative several of his grandpa's tall tales. This had been accomplished in such a skilled manner that Blackbourne had contrived to sound like a lifelong friend.

Equally graceful he proved to be at returning survivors to the prosaic world. At the judicious moment, his gravity turned jocular. He winked at Saber and angled his broad face to indicate Felicity's blossoming belly.

"Young man, we all travel through this vale with too little understanding of the whys and wherefores of the journey. But as an outsider, may I suggest that your grandfather was content to leave knowing that another was ready to take his place in this world? It's a thought worth pondering."

He drew Saber aside a step and spoke with deep sincerity.

"You let Mr. Fielding know I took good care of you and yours, hear?" At Saber's nod, he continued, "I've tried to tell the old coot to listen to good sense and get out of the way of you up-and-comers. He's too old-fashioned for the modern mining business. So next time you see him, you remind him that Able's got a place for him." He winked again, this time solemnly. "At the country club on weekday mornings. Golf, you know."

They shook hands. Saber took Felicity's arm as they descended the carpeted steps.

"I love you," she whispered, bestowing on him a fleeting kiss as he helped her into their new car. It was a red and white Oldsmobile, and she was as happy as a June bug on May thirty-first as she settled awkwardly into the vinyl-covered front seat.

Saber paused as he opened his own door. In this old area of the city the residences were like mansions, three stories tall with shutters and gables and ornate woodwork and stained glass and wrought iron fences. The sidewalks were slate. Oak trees gaunt and damp with snow looked down on children's tricycles and luxury automobiles, symbols of the coming and going of generations. The formless grey of the wintery sky itself seemed to express timelessness in the face of change.

But Saber discovered himself responding with an affect he found vaguely disquieting. It was the same emotion that had troubled him when he told Felicity about his childhood. He didn't know what it meant or why he felt it. It always began in the pit of his stomach, too sudden to guard against. It always ended as a sickness of heart, fading too quickly to identify.

19

He gunned the engine, and the heater fan blasted frigid air. Felicity gasped and Saber shoved the knob in with a flash of irritation.

He shifted the automatic transmission and pulled from the curb. He checked the rear-view mirror one more time. As he did, he thought he saw a slim figure slip behind one of the trees.

*

Four years of applying modern business theory with his innate acumen brought Saber rapidly up the rungs of the Fielding Mining Corporation. The core business of the staid corporation was lease-operating hundreds of natural gas wells along the Rockies. These generated enormous profits, such that the penny-pinching Fielding had accumulated two hundred million in cash reserves. But with so many of the leases expiring and a certainty they would be expensive to renew, Fielding tasked Saber with diversifying the business.

Saber acted with daring. He bought from receivership a silver-zinc mine in California and a copper-molybdenum mine in Arizona and recapitalized them. He took ownership of a soda ash operation in Wyoming and fired its management, subsequently doubling its productivity. He employed a broker in South Africa and began importing manganese and chromium.

Even during dreams Saber's mind swirled with images of mines and molten metals. It was more as an afterthought that he purchased the oil drilling options on a Colorado tract. The underground pool of oil turned out to be a lake. Fielding celebrated the success with a company dinner and dubbed him with title of junior vice-president. In a whirlwind of mergers and acquisitions, Saber absorbed electric utilities across Colorado, Iowa, Kansas, Nebraska, and South Dakota, and fed their power plants with oil from Fielding wells.

Titans of the mining industry were stunned by this vertical integration of mining and energy, but when word spread that the Fielding Corporation planned to venture into coal mining, they scoffed. It was common knowledge that there were no undiscovered coal fields on the continent, and that coal companies were already mining whatever could be easily accessed. As for the huge coal fields of the Powder

River Basin in Wyoming and the mountaintop seams in Appalachia, sinking shafts in them wouldn't allow extraction at competitive prices.

But Saber spurned conventional wisdom. His drive had become an unstoppable force. He found a firm in Germany that had designed mechanical leviathans called bucket wheel excavators, and ordered one. Longer than two football fields and twenty stories high, the ten-thousand ton machine could fill several trains with coal in a day. With the monstrous excavator chugging away, the Powder River Basin would produce coal so cheaply that no one could compete with it.

Nor were the Appalachian mountaintops safe.

"We'll use dynamite to blow the top of the mountain off," he told Felicity. "Bring in bulldozers and shove all the debris—trees and rocks and dirt—into ravines and hollows. When the seam is exposed, we'll scrape as deep as we can with earthmovers. Then we dynamite again, repeating the process. We dig down and down until there's no mountain left."

Felicity pursed her lips, watching herself roll the curlers into her hair. After a while she glanced at Saber in the vanity mirror. "Sweetie, you don't really think the hillbillies living on those mountains are going to let you do that, do you?"

He wondered at her naivite. "Heck, Felicity," he said. "No more shafts and cave-ins, no more drilling, no more miners and no more union rules. The coal will be practically free. There'll be enough grease for everyone's palms. We'll buy out the hillbillies and they'll move to different mountains with cash in their pockets. There isn't any shortage of mountains. "

Felicity turned and stared at him. Finally she said, "Will you get a raise out of this? I simply must have a housekeeper."

An empire is expensive to maintain, Fielding soon discovered. Saber's acquisitions over several years were so inspired that the entire mining industry was beset with turmoil. Nevertheless, Fielding finally called Saber to his office and bade him postpone further diversification until cash flow caught up with expenditures. The reserves were drained and every penny of profits coming in had to be spent for capital improvements of the new operations. The bucket wheel excavator still hadn't arrived, equipment at the mines was being modernized, three power plants were shut down for repairs, and nuisance lawsuits temporarily halted the mountaintop removals in Kentucky. While the soda ash subsidiary and the importing division turned profits, their gross sales only constituted a small part of the business. It was the natural gas wells that kept the company in the black, and their long-term leases were coming due for renewal.

In Saber's imagination, the order couldn't have come at a worse time. He closed up the tables and charts and research papers he had been studying for the last three months and gloomily headed for home.

He dutifully stopped at the post office and sent the usual monthly check to his pappy.

Only one man had climbed the ladder as fast as Saber, and he always stayed one rung ahead of him. The wily Carl Warner, ten years his senior, had left the Department of the Interior to make his fortune in private industry. Opportunistic and quick-thinking, he was adept at endorsing Saber's maneuvers staunchly enough to claim credit if they succeeded while remaining blameless if they should fail. The two men had ambition in common, so their mutual wariness precluded amity. But when Warner was laying groundwork for an executive coup d'etat, he began cultivating Saber as an ally.

"You'll become senior vice-president," Warner promised, "and no one knows better than I do that you've earned the title, as well as the perquisites that go with it."

A short step from being the youngest president-CEO in the industry, Saber thought. He mused whether there was any way to make Warner tumble at the same time Fielding himself did.

"You want to mine uranium," Warner said, and gave him a wink. "Shhh, it's just our secret. You, me, and Sandra in the mail room." He showed off the gap in his front teeth with a broad smile. "And Fielding won't let you. But it's the right thing to do."

Warner steered Saber down the hall toward his corner office.

"The Atomic Energy Commission," he said, closing the door behind them, "is buying all the uranium it can get its hands on, so we'll have no problem selling it. We're in the atomic age. Atomic bombs, submarines, reactors. Atomic cars, atomic kitchens, who knows? But none of it happens without uranium. And Fielding..." Warner paused and smoothed his slim Ernie Kovacs moustache. He narrowed his eyes. "You're a college boy. You see where I'm going with this? If at the next stockholder meeting I propose we get into uranium mining, what do you figure will happen?"

"Fielding will blow his stack," Saber said. "We'd have to borrow to do it, and the old man hates debt. So he'll denounce the idea. But the shareholders will love it."

Warner grinned.

"Hell, yes. Fielding stock will jump a dollar a share just by announcing it. And the Board will realize that Fielding is a dinosaur, which they've suspected for years. They put him out to pasture, and we go borrow in the capital markets with a sure thing. You are indeed one smart cookie, which is why I want you on my side."

Saber mentally shrugged off the flattery. Warner didn't really need an ally for his presentation to the Board. Warner needed him for quite another reason. Government geological surveys had located dozens of promising uranium sites across Wyoming, but mineral rights to most had been secured by other mining companies.

Some of the richest ores, however, were directly under the hardscrabble ranch of Sam Drecker. And old man Drecker took potshots at fancy-talking lawyers with his gopher rifle. He would deal with no one but Saber.

Saber and Warner hand-shook the deal, and Saber put a call through to Sam Drecker.

That afternoon driving home, he counted eight long-skirted teenaged girls out in front of suburban tract homes rotating their skinny hips in plastic hula hoops, and twenty-five teenaged boys playing catch with plastic discs that resembled flying saucers. It brought to his mind the parade sword that he had wielded so innocently and manfully, and again the brief sense of heartsickness crept over him.

On Saturday he shopped the local dealer for a Thunderbird, chose one, and drove it home for Felicity to agree with. On the new four-lane bypass he tapped the accelerator, testing the enormous horsepower of the V-8, and decided he was happy, after all.

*

With his accession to second-in-command, Saber's life achieved a sunny plateau of satisfaction. Felicity presented him with another child, this one a bubbly blonde daughter to match his rambunctious blond son, and he was elected to the Chamber of Commerce board. In winter, he and Felicity and the children flew on TWA Airlines to Miami and ponied up for the brand-new experience of an in-flight movie. In spring, Saber hired an architect to draw up plans for a ranch home well outside the suburban sprawl. A man hardly older than himself was President of the nation, another ambitious upstart helping to write a new chapter of history, and with this new hero Saber felt a satisfying kinship. He had steered them through the treacherous waters of a nuclear-armed Cuba. Now he reassured them that not even outer space would pose a limitation on what modern man could accomplish. And while astronauts trained, Saber would plumb the earth for the uranium to fuel that great cosmic voyage. The icing on the cake of Saber's success took the form of an elfin new personal secretary whose dark eyes shone with age-old passion.

Her name was Claudia. In the office she anticipated his expectations before he voiced them. In conferences she was subtle, at the water cooler discreet. In bed she moved like an animal.

All the questions that Felicity had once asked about his childhood, Claudia asked as well. But while Felicity's questions arose out of her simple ardor, Claudia's were asked with a probing feline curiosity that at once left him defenseless and mesmerized. Yet his memories of poverty and neglect, when revealed to Claudia, seemed ennobling more than shameful. The rough mountainside turned into an enchanted kingdom.

"Your grandfather loved you very much," she told him matter-of-factly.

"I suppose he did," Saber said, stunned by the notion.

When the heroic young President was assassinated, it was Claudia who assuaged his grief. She had been taking his dictation when the news was piped in on the PA system. Shutting her steno pad, Claudia locked the office door and came around the desk to his side. Standing close beside him, she hugged his head against her breasts while he cried. Then with smooth and unhurried grace, she slipped her panties down over her ankles and climbed astride his lap.

That was the only time she let him have her in the office. Sensitive to her professional position, any other times Claudia locked the door were for his benefit alone.

Saber scorned the moptop haircuts appearing on young men, but Claudia undermined this prejudice. She persuaded him to let his own thinning locks lengthen over the collar.

"She says it's more harmonious with nature," he complained to Warner.

In the beginning, he once mentioned her to Felicity.

"I meant to tell you," he said, as he carved into the chestnut-sauced turkey he favored for Easter, "we hired a new secretary for the office. Pleasant enough girl, except that she advises me to dress more modernly."

Felicity poured glasses of Tang for the children and didn't even give him a glance.

"Sweetie," she said, "you know the rule about discussing the office at home."

He took Felicity to a new movie on her birthday. It fell on an evening that he usually worked late with Claudia.

"I don't understand this at all," Felicity groaned, halfway through George C. Scott's memorable harangue. As it was the premier of the controversial "Dr. Strangelove," the theater was capacity crowd. Their children were being babysat, and even Saber's hand stroking Felicity's thigh didn't quell her sighs of annoyance. So it happened that Felicity had retired to the concession stand for a Coke when the big bomb was rodeo-ridden to earth and the billowing nuclear fungus climbed into the heavens on its monstrous stalk.

Saber stared with horror that had hidden behind his life and was now revealed in the blackest comedy. The assassination of the young President had been only a foretaste of the pall darkening the world. No one again in history would live a hundred-forty years. No one.

25

He knew that with the same prickling conviction that he knew the young woman down front, who had turned in her seat to gaze speculatively at him, was Claudia.

*

Warner's triumphant reign turned out to be an interregnum. The Fielding Corporation quite suddenly found itself being overbid on renewal of their natural gas leases, despite specializing in running such wells profitably. Saber and Warner spent long days together with their production engineers, slicing their margins then slashing them, but to no avail. Every bid, even those offered in desperation at the cost of production, was beaten by a competitor. Together they poured over accounting and invoices and systems charts until the hateful hours of the morning when they would be snarling at each other. They could find nowhere to cut overhead. Meanwhile, the deterioration of cash flow imperiled their short-term debt structure. Warner let go assistant managers and a third of the engineers, and began to underbid even his own cost projections.

"We'll ride it out," he assured Saber one evening as he worked on his fourth martini. They had abandoned their efforts early and retired to the club lounge. "Everyone who's beaten our bids has to be losing their shirts. It's a kamikaze war, a bloodbath. Someone will go under, and everybody else'll wake up."

"The uranium move overextended us. We'll be the odd man out." Saber parked his elbows on the mahogany bar and clasped his face. "My methods revolutionized mining, doubling and tripling output, and every company but ours will profit from it."

"You're wrong. The uranium will be exactly what saves us. We'll be shipping very soon. We can hang on until then."

"And what happens," Saber said, lifting his head to gaze flatly at Warner, "if the price of uranium drops?"

At the beginning of the next year, the price paid for uranium plummeted. The boom upon which capitalization had been predicated went bust. The Drecker uranium mining was closed down, their marginal utilities were liquidated, and the bucket wheel excavator was sold to a competitor to pay down debts. The wrath of the Board of Directors swept Warner into early retirement. Saber was suspected of sharing blame for the debacle, but his presence in the executive suite was needed to maintain stock market confidence. The Board reluctantly voted him in as president.

Meanwhile, Felicity underwent a hysterectomy for a benign condition in her female apparatus. She began to sigh a lot and watch soap operas on their RCA color television. One morning at breakfast Saber realized he felt neither love nor passion for her, and as she became a stranger to him, his children also became strangers to him.

He was stunned when she gave him the news. Claudia had closed the door of the office and curled her slim figure into the chair where she usually took dictation. She informed him of her condition in the fewest possible words, and with her usual aplomb.

"How many months along?" he asked, as he emerged from his initial stupefaction.

With a wide smile, she said, "A lot."

"Good lord, you're going to have it?"

Claudia gave a slight shrug with her thin square shoulders. It was a shrug of assent, not doubt. She repositioned herself in the chair, straightening up and putting her hands in her lap. Saber suddenly realized that what he had noticed when she was last naked with him, but had left unconsidered, was true. Her breasts had grown. They were like heavy ripe fruit yearning to burst her blouse, promising gratification of all hungers, physical and existential. He blinked away the image.

"We were making a baby," Claudia said reasonably. "Why are you surprised?"

"We were having a goddamned affair!" he retorted. "I have a family! I have friends and neighbors! I'm president of the third largest mining company in America!"

After a few moments he calmed. He leaned back in his chair and sighed.

"I can never acknowledge it's mine," he said.

She stared off to the left, warily licking her lips.

"You don't have to. I'll leave."

"There's no alternative. We have a company rule about out-of-wedlock pregnancies."

"I meant leave you," she said.

Saber began frantically running his fingers through his stylishly-cut hair. Never once during his infrequent reflections on the future of the affair had the possibility occurred to him that Claudia might end it. She had no interest in other men, and her enthusiasm for being pleased by him was as boundless as her talents at pleasing him were impassioned. Suddenly the hollowness of every other aspect of his life struck him to the core.

"I'm in love with you, Claudia," he said. He said it without thinking, but as the words left his lips he realized nothing could have been more profoundly truthful.

"I have to go, Saber. This mining business is barbaric." She tilted her head as if to give him a new perspective on herself. Then she laughed gaily in the way he adored, displaying her perfect white teeth, and added with feeling, "But I got more pleasure from you than I ever imagined!"

When she unwound her legs from beneath her and rose, Saber gazed steadily at her.

"How will I know where to find you?"

She paused on her way to the door. Smoothing her skirt across her belly, she looked down at herself for a moment or two.

"You should forget, and I should forget," she said solemnly. "Our baby should be the only memory of what happened between us."

*

Carl Warner devoted his ample leisure time to golfing, and occasionally Saber made a fourth for the threesome of the wily Warner, taciturn Fielding, and affable Blackbourne. Their male comraderie was cemented in unspoken ties, but Saber sometimes felt that they kept him at a distance. It was as if they had all surrendered to some terrible inevitability and made an awkward peace with it, while he himself was yet struggling against it. They seemed to secretly resent him, even while they were backslapping.

Saber discovered there was some measure of truth to this reckoning in a particularly vivid fashion. Carl Warner was invited for dinner on Saber and Felicity's anniversary. Felicity prepared and served roasted pork basted with blackberry jam. After dessert the nanny shepherded the children away while the grown-ups sipped brandy and discussed the state of the world.

"The problem," Warner was saying, "is that no one respects their obligations anymore. To be sure, we all want freedom, but freedom comes with a price tag. Take free love, for example. That's a social abomination, as if we're no better than rutting beasts in the forest. It was the beatniks who invented that idea."

Warner was, Saber presumed, leading up to his most recent pet peeve, the free speech movement on the nation's campuses. His expectation wasn't confirmed, because Felicity got it into her head to pursue the tangent.

"Carl, what does an upstanding man like you know about beatniks and free love? Are you patronizing those coffeehouses at the university?"

"Well!" Warner chuckled. "I admit I'm not as experienced as your husband."

"Oh?" Felicity set her elbows on the table and turned to Saber with a look of mock suspicion.

"He's trying to make you jealous, Felice. Pay him no mind at all."

Saber shot Warner a warning glance, which Warner cheerfully ignored. He reached over and patted Felicity's hand.

"Don't worry your pretty little head, my dear. He's on the straight and narrow path. His office door is always open, now that..." Warner caught himself in time.

"Not at the dinner table," Felicity said crisply.

Misconstruing her meaning, Warner breathed a relieved sigh.

"Thank God," he said, wiping his brow. "For a second there I thought I'd let the cat out of the bag."

Felicity glanced at Saber with confusion. An instant later her eyes grew wide with enlightenment, and she looked down at her brandy as they narrowed with hatred. With the equanimity of an executive's wife, she excused herself and went to the bathroom to cry.

Warner and Saber retreated to the open porch. Warner offered him a Honduran cigar, accompanying it with an uninteresting lament about the Cuban embargo. They puffed in the earthy quiet of the night. From out in the flats came the modulated roar of teenaged drag racing. The amber glow of Denver arched over half the horizon as if conquering the heart of darkness.

Finally Saber cleared his throat.

"It's all going to hell, Carl." His voice was husky.

"Not the marriage?" Warned sounded truly chagrined.

"That, too, I suppose. But what I meant was the world." He held his cigar out with a straight arm and tapped ashes into the rose bushes. "The planet."

"Nahh." Carl Warner's thin lips turned down at the corners, dragging his narrow moustache with them. Lines creased his jowls, and Saber noticed how much retirement had aged him. "Every generation gets to thinking that after a while. It goes with the territory. It happens when you realize that your big plans were just a lot of hooey."

Suddenly Saber felt a great sadness for this man whose dream had been reduced to achieving par on a nine-hole golf course.

"It's worse for our generation, Carl. For a few years there we had the power to make this world a better place. And what'd we do? We started an arms race with the Russians and turned the world into a ticking time bomb that can't ever be disarmed. Why'd we do that? Who'd we do it for? Not our wives and children. I'm looking to you for words of wisdom, not homilies. You've had time to think while you were putting that stupid ball around. Why'd we do it, Carl? You tell me."

Warner's face appeared tired and frightened in the porchlight.

"I don't know, Saber. That's the truth. I don't know."

Saber nodded reflectively. "Neither do I," he said.

The very next day, Fielding suffered a fatal stroke while golfing with Blackbourne. He died on the last hole. It was simultaneous with Felicity arriving at her lawyer's to request a divorce on grounds of adultery, and only a few minutes before Carl Warner parked his white convertible Eldorado in the Fielding Mining Corporation parking lot and rode up to the fourteenth floor. He stood at the window of his old office, gazed for the last time at the Denver skyline, aimed a snubnose .32 at his right temple, and fired a shot.

Saber himself was the first to his side. Later, after the police had questioned him, he left the Fielding building and never returned. Day after day he sat alone in the lounge of the country club, getting drunk in a corner booth, trying to decide whether he could visit his children without armfuls of presents. In the end he concluded he couldn't. He sold his stock, signed a quit claim on the house after paying off the mortgage, and boarded a Greyhound bus for home.

*

His tired legs carried him up the winding dirt road from the highway, and sweat made his dusty clothes cling to his skin by the time he reached the rutted driveway ascending to his childhood home. The clapboards were grey with only flecks of paint remaining. The roof sagged near the chimney. He didn't remember if it always had. And his pappy was sitting on the porch swing, in remarkable likeness to his grandpa.

Through the stifling afternoon they drank beer from cans, sitting side by side on the porch. They were unpracticed at father and son conversation, but each was willing to let the other speak for a spell and listen disinterestedly until it was his own turn to talk. The older man reminisced about a meteor shower so bright it alarmed the rooster to crowing, and about the snake that fell down the chimney, and about the birth of a two-headed baby to Sam Drecker's youngest granddaughter. When it came his turn, Saber talked about the new war in Indochina, and about electronic machines that replaced clerical workers, and about California wines that rivalled fermented blackberry juice.

His pappy crushed the last empty beer can and made a disgusted comment about the new aluminum alloys. He tossed it overhead into the ragweed where the other cans had ended up. They went inside.

"Got an extra tv dinner here if you want, Say."

Saber declined.

"Had to get electricity after Joe quit delivering coal. Got the 'lectric stove here from Sam Drecker. He bought a new range. Don't mind progress so much sometimes." He studied the box containing the pre-made meal. "Don't mind the fact of refrigeration, but I mind the fact of tv. Progress didn't do much for us there, did it, now? Sam got it. He got himself a tv as big as a hogshead. Now he's got no interest in pinouchle, not even horseshoes."

After years of eking out a living on reluctant land, his pappy had arthritic hands. He weighed the packaged dinner in his gnarled fist as if he wanted to smash it on something, and abruptly turned on Saber.

"Where's your family, anyways?" he demanded. "Where's my little grandkids? That the way grown-ups in the city do it? Walk off and that's it? Why, why..." He threw the tv dinner down on the bare table. "Glad your grandpa's not here, to see you with nothing to show for your smarts but a city suit and more'n your fair share of dollars."

Saber stood at the screen door and inhaled the twilight air. His pappy fiddled with the electric stove and frowned at the package instructions.

"Think I'll take a walk around, Pap. See what they did to Drecker's ridge."

"Nothing to see up there," came the bitter reply. "Lotta mud. Even the wolfthing went away."

Saber took his time going down the lane, smoking a Viceroy cigarette that was the last of the pack he'd bought for the bus trip. He paused by the watering trough, now entirely hidden from view by wild rye, and then angled up the rocky path toward the ridge.

The copse of cottonwoods was now gone. In its place was a bleak graveyard of machine parts already rusting in a clearing of dry clay. Saber climbed onward, grasping branches now and again to get himself up the steep trail in his wingtips.

When he reached the ridge, he followed the trail along it until he could peer down into the hollow. The chokecherry trees there had also been uprooted and carted away to allow passage for the Caterpillar earthmovers. A makeshift road ran like a cruel gash through the forlorn hollow. The cattails and milkweed by the creek wouldn't flourish again, not with the topsoil gone. Only pale clay remained. It would bake and crack in the summer, and turn to muck in the rain, staining the sneakers of any boy who might be exploring.

Saber continued on. He didn't know what he was looking for, and what he saw didn't affect him, because he was beyond caring. The harsh invasion of progress had despoiled the mountainside where he once played, but Saber felt neither guilt nor sorrow. He felt only indifferent curiosity.

Sam Drecker's rambling home still perched on the outcropping where it had sat for a half-century, but it was dark now and lifeless. From this elevation, Saber could glimpse the new Drecker split-level ranch house. It was farther along the mountain, but even at its great distance the flickering illumination of television shone through the windows.

He walked forward into the expanse that had once been undulating wooded ranchland. After a few paces he halted. The moon was high above him, fuller than a dead yellow cat on the highway, and it cast a clinical light on the appalling horror of the open-pit uranium mine. For a mile in front of him stretched an immense gruesome ulcer, gouged into earth like a hellish stadium, with mangled shrubbery and trees bulldozed into mounds along its perimeter. An eerie silence prevailed.

This is what we have done, Saber thought. And in time the whole planet would look like this, while people huddled in ranch homes bathed in the glow of television. Cities would be fat throbbing pustules on the utter desolation. Nature herself would perish.

Saber slowly sat down in the clay and crossed his legs. A quarter hour passed before he noticed the shape of a young woman crouched on a felled tree, near the boundary of the bleak expanse. Her knees were drawn up to her breasts, her fists were bracing herself on the tree trunk, and her eyes were watching him keenly.

He rose and dusted off the seat of his slacks and walked in her direction. She had in her eyes the same speculative glitter as in the movie theater after the Strangelove bomb had fallen. A cosmic clarity exploded through his supreme indifference, and it dispelled the perplexion that hounded him. All the niggling questions that could have sprung to his mind still hovered unspoken, but he understood that their separate answers did not matter, that everything together made sense.

When he was close enough, she dropped from her perch and met him nakedly with a small purr. They stood pressed together, face to face, arms at their sides. The top of her head fitted under his chin, her hardened nipples pressed against his chest, and her earthy musk, mingling with the scent of blackberries in her hair, filled his nostrils. He felt her giggle.

"Oh, I can see you even now, charging up the path with that silly old sword." She cocked her head so she could look up at him. "And running so fast I could never catch you. I wouldn't have harmed you, just taught you my ways. But a saber slashes its way through the world, doesn't it?"

Her hands at her sides moved slightly forward, so that her fingertips grazed his. She was still talking into his chest, and he felt her words as much as he heard them.

"I missed you so much when you went away. I waited and waited and waited for you to come back. When your grandpa left, I followed him. I saw you with that woman you married, driving in a brand new car. So I knew you weren't ever coming back, and I gave up and came home. And then you sent men and machines here. Awful, awful noise, day and night, buzzing and pounding and scraping and shouting back and forth. All the other animals ran away. I had nothing to eat. And I was afraid. Those men would have caught me and done horrible things to me."

Gripping his forearms, she leaned back to search his face.

"So I learned to practice deceit."

"You came to Denver to work for us," he said, with the wondrous clarity focusing into distinct understandings. "You leaked our bids. You gave them to our competitors. They took their turns overbidding, so none of them would bleed too much while our company hemorrhaged."

"You should have left me alone."

"We needed the uranium," he said, faintly.

"But you were destroying my world, Saber."

He thought about the silvery Strangelove bomb descending through the air toward the green and blue planet. He thought about

34

golf clubs and cigars and parade swords, and he thought about guided missiles and gopher rifles and revolvers, and he thought about the relentless drilling and pumping and shafting of the earth by the mining companies. More than anything he wanted to ask her the same question he had asked Warner, at the fateful dinner, but the answer was too obvious to deny. And too late, because the damage he had caused was too profound.

She pressed herself hard against him, and they embraced with the tenderness that only two ex-lovers can achieve, and then only briefly.

"Did you see what you did to my lovely hollow?" she murmured.

He could hear the mewling of her newborn nearby. He tried to look once more at her elfin face, but tears in his eyes made everything a blur.

"I wish," she whispered, "you hadn't been so afraid of me." Her extraordinary pelvis tightened to his, grinding seductively, and she gave a low and resonant hum while kissing her soft lips along his throat.

"I'm not afraid anymore," he said, with a catch in his voice.

He didn't even flinch as the wolfthing wrapped her arms over his shoulders, clawing at the nape of his neck with hungry abandon. Her hum abruptly became a feline snarl, and, opening her beautiful mouth very wide, she sank her teeth deep in his throat and pulled him bloody and unresisting to the waiting earth.

About the Visitor from Anotherworld

(In response to current speculation and inquiries, this memorandum has been composed at the desk of Solomon the 342nd.)

"Gimme a pigsfoot and aaaa bottle o' beer..." the sailor trilled as they marched him into court. And not unmelodiously, considering his hard salt appearance.

Or so I mused. The jurors thought otherwise and with less jurisprudence.

"Send him to the gallows!" they howled.

The poor fellow halted in mid-verse, bewildered by the malice. I clammered my hammer and began the proceedings.

"Karma court in session," I declared. "The past is the future of the present!"

They all echoed this statement in a booming but incomprehensible chorus. The sailor stared out at the millions of televideo faces and cocked his head in confusion.

"Isn't the present the past of the future?" he asked.

"Heresy!" an expert psychic witness shrieked, and the multitudinous jury turned it into a chant.

As Solomon, I was obliged to intervene.

"Hear his piteous tale!" I demanded, clammering my hammer again. "Follow your leader and sport the court!"

"No more sillies!" they roared.

"Stop it! Stop it! Stop it!" I warned. "Or be penalized a hundred lives over!"

That quelled the outbursts for the moment. But as soon as he took his defense, which was no defense at all, he clenched a fist and shook it at the masses with foolhardy defiance.

"Send me back to Anotherworld! I'm a free man!"

He was regaled with jeers. "Fry the spy!" and "Drown the clown!"

Something must be done, I thought, but with that din I could hardly hear myself think it.

"Remember and regret!" I barked. "The way back is the way forward!"

The millions chorused it to me reluctantly.

"New session tomorrow!" I declared, and court disbanded.

"Solomon Incarnate the 342nd at your service," I identified myself to him as we walked together past slumstreet shanties. "Prepared to dispense your best advice."

Televideo waves wafted through the hot afternoon air. I took him down through the dusty piazza where gangly girls fed their ice cream cones to frolicking yellow dogs, and nut-brown boys roughhoused with the game of slap-me-sorry. The afternoon was full of fine penance.

"Don't like it here," he mumbled over and over, until at last I asked him why not.

"Well, what's the point, matey?"

"Come along and you'll see," I assured him.

We crossed the bridge. As we passed the river's midpoint, the surface shimmered. When the liquacious distortions cleared, shantytown had vanished from view. The sailor gasped in alarm and swung around, but of course there was nothing behind but blue sky and cottonball clouds over a silvery ocean. He pointed a gnarled finger at where shantytown had been. His mouth opened to speak but he was at a loss for words.

Gripping his sinewy arm, I escorted him toward the Grand Plaza, where in alabaster hotels celebrities played dice with fate. We toured while karma stars in full loveliness groaned and hurrahed with their luck. I swept my arm over the glorious sight.

"Don't you want to someday be one of the privileged? Get it together and spend the rest of your life here?"

He turned to me, aghast.

"I only want to go home," he insisted.

"There's no return from now," I reminded him.

"This is a *here*, not a *now*," he objected. "And I want to return from *here*, not from *now*."

I favored him with a benign smile.

"But *here* is *now*," I said. "*There* was *then*, and you can't go back."

The mariner clapped his calloused hands on my shoulders and squeezed them.

"Matey! Even if we're *here-now* and Anotherworld was *there-then*, surely there must be a *there-now*, and I want to be *there-then*. And you'll have no more trouble from me."

He stared into my face as if begging me to understand. What I did understand was that it wasn't some dread guilt he sought to conceal. He was simply too naïve for that.

"I'm sure you don't mean to disrupt the judicial process," I said, generously allowing him the benefit of any doubt. "But a man can't shirk his penitential duties. We want what's best for you, isn't that plain to see?"

"Look, Solomon Incarnate," he said, and offered me his hand. "It's been most genuine, the pleasure of this conversation, but methinks the tide ebbs for you and me."

"Not just yet," said I.

I led him outside, where it was sunset and a glorious one. From the beach hurried a tide of lobster-red couples carrying picnic leftovers. Those who were the most sunburned wore grim looks of self-satisfaction. We struggled the wrong way against the crush of bodies.

"Damned lemmings," the sailor muttered.

"Lemmings also seek nirvana," I countered, "and they plunge off the cliff in pursuit of it. There can't be progress without penance. All events are connected in time."

"But what if mine aren't connected to yours?" he wanted to know. "You plan to lock me up forever and ever, matey?"

"What else?" I asked. "How can you gain redemption without making amends?"

"It's nothing I have to be guilty of!" he cried. "It's an honest life that I've lived!"

"And the lives before this one? Do you think the world forgets those?"

He stared at me, befuddled. "You've lost me there, matey," he said, and turned toward the ocean with visible longing.

I tossed a few pebbles into the water. The waves cast them back and we had to duck.

"No going back," I explained to him. "Neither you nor the pebbles. There's no hope but to repent and atone."

The visitor took a glistening pebble and tried it himself. He dodged the incoming.

"Bet you used to play this game when you were young," he said. "Didn't you?"

"I grew up in Anotherworld. Stones skip there." He frowned at the burnished gold of the horizon. "Tell me, mate, when's the trial over? Five minutes a day gets you nowhere, when you think about it."

"How can we have an end, if we have nowhere to start?"

This truthful nugget he mulled over with a frown. His sunburned visage was etched with lined maps of his years at sea.

"So I should tell all?"

"And leave nothing unimportant out."

"I was born on a fair day on a fair isle and walked on sea legs before I had whiskers," he began the next day. "As to how I sailed my vessel into your world, it's more a puzzle to me than to you. Blame it on fickle winds, but it isn't my fault, mateys. I plead an injustice has been done. Acquit me."

They howled bitterly, the millions.

"That's the extent of the story?" I asked in disbelief, shocked he'd cheat them that way.

"All else is but a tale of rough seas, empty sails, and cheating women," he asided to me, but the microphone picked it up and the millions heard.

40

"Hekyll and Jekyll!" they jeered. "Jekyll and Hyde!"

I gazed at him in exasperation and he gazed back, plainly confused.

"You see," I said. "They doubt your sainthood."

"But I told it from the start!"

"Back up!" the millions chorused.

"To where?" Now he seemed terrified. "Ill winds blew me here instead of my destination in Anotherworld! What's previous, mateys?"

"The beginning and middle!" they chanted, loud and clear. "The beginning and middle!"

"No progress without regress," I explained. "Nothing in the world just happens."

"Well, then," he said, faltering, but choosing to brazen it out. "God was playing croquet when me mum prays to him, see, and says to give her a winsome baby girl. Well, God was about to make a shot just then and win the game, 'cause being omnipotent and all He must win or else. The world would crumble, you see?"

The masses were quiet now, attentive to every syllable. He grew in confidence and ran the game to its limit.

"So, mateys, God gave the right instructions, but He was also concentrating on His shot, and was subsequently and consequently misinterpreted by His angels. Me mum didn't dare complain." He surveyed the millions of the jury and took a deep breath. "So as it happens, I'm here as direct result of the fact that God had the balls but didn't take the time, me mum took the time but didn't have the balls, and so I wound up with balls in no time at all!"

He looked about triumphantly. The jury was speechless for a moment before one ancient soothsayer in front hissed, "Fruitcake."

Thereupon a storm of shouts descended from all directions and all walks of life.

"Cement his feet! Drop him in the deep!" And so on.

Tears welled in his eyes and trickled down his cheeks.

"I lied, matey, didn't I?"

"That's the spirit," I murmured.

It was my guess (or so I scribbled in the margins of the trial transcript) that the poor man had no understanding of spiritual evolution.

It seemed that he was somehow handicapped in that regard. For who could not know his own previousness? Who could absolve himself of that burden, except one bereft of the faculty for remembering it? The sailor knew nothing of his karma. He suffered from a cruel form of idiocy and deserved pity more than punishment. Because, although ignorance is criminal and incompetence doesn't equal innocence, there are sometimes circumstances that call for compassion.

A final ruling was withheld. Without previousness, how could we judge? And so, lest he by odd mischance propagate, burdening society with more misfits incapable of grasping their own past lives, he was summarily vasectomized.

We issued him a false past and urged him to memorize it well. After scuttling his vessel, we released him on probation. He returned of his own accord not a week later.

"Can't bear it," he confessed. "Magic bridges and mumbling martyrs, and with a wrong word or gesture demerits dispensed like candy. All disincentive and nothing spontaneous, you got that? Lock me up forever and ever til I die."

"That's no solution," I reminded him. "We'd have to lock you up again next time, and so on for eternity."

"Then what am I to do," he wept, "with no crimes to regret or promises to keep? Can't stay, can't hide, and can't escape! Oh, for Anotherworld!"

"Are you sure there is one?" I asked a bit sharply, for I was losing my patience.

"There can't be," he moaned. "If there was, where could it have come from?"

"Now you're learning," I said.

"I'm talking like you," he sniffled. "I'm even thinking like you, matey. But that doesn't give me a past."

Then I had the wondrous epiphany for which I'll ever be remembered.

"Maybe you're at the beginning," I whispered.

He wiped his eyes and looked up hopefully. "So I had no past?"

Heresy! And yet suppose some soul had attained glorious nirvana and now his place was being taken by a fresh new soul? What about my predecessor, Solomon the 341st? Yes, the number of years since his demise matched closely with this poor fool's age! I could sell it to the millions and dismiss the case!

"But," I said, "you aren't altogether lucky with that explanation. What are you going to do with yourself if you have nothing to repent, no remorse to suffer, no redemption to seek? Terrible but true, eh?"

He stared about desperately. Suddenly he seized my secretary, who had been responsibly taking notes, and heaved her out the window to her death.

"Now I do!" he chortled.

At the new trial he received a standing ovation. He took to the stage like a homecoming hero, and I knew for certain all was well. He had found his place in the future. I knew that, because I looked forward to meeting with him again in a future incarnation. The finer ladies seemed to feel the same. I noticed a number of them dabbing handkerchiefs to their eyes as we lopped off his head.

"That's progress!" everybody shouted enthusiastically, and I went down in history, as you already know, for my marvelous insight and wisdom.

THE KID WHO COULDN'T SLEEP

Cast of Characters

KID, a ten-year old boy grappling with awareness of mortality
VISITORS:
> GRIM REAPER, young version of Mr. Death
> GIRL, young version of woman KID will marry
> DAD, young version of KID's father
> MOM, young version of KID's mother
> ALEXANDER THE GREAT, young version of same
> MOZART, young version of same
> MAN, ninety-three year old version of the KID

SCENE 1

At RISE:

> (The late 1980's. A darkened bedroom
> with a bed, dresser, desk and chair. KID is
> in bed in his pajamas, awake.)

> KID

What if I don't grow up?

> (Sits straight up and turns the light on.)

45

I'm ten! What if I don't get to be eleven? What if I don't even get to be here tomorrow?

(Falls back on his pillow. Turns light off.)

GRIM REAPER
(Voice in dark.)

That's right, kid. What if you don't get to see the bright and shining sun come up in the morning? What if you don't get to be a teenager racing up and down the streets in your dad's Chevy? What if you don't meet the pretty girl you think you will and what if you don't have kids of your own? But what if you do? What do you think happens after all that, anyway?

KID
(In a small voice.)

What?

GRIM REAPER

You die.

KID
(Now in a scared voice.)

Dad?

GRIM REAPER

Guess again.

KID

Mom?

GRIM REAPER

Oh, sure!

KID

You're not really there, are you?

GRIM REAPER

Of course I'm here. I'm everywhere. I'm here, I'm there, I'm down at the mall, I'm on a airplane at the airport, I'm riding at the country club. Of course, I'm usually uninvited. But I get in without invitations. Doors don't keep me out, burglar alarms don't go off, police don't come until it's too late. Wanna take another guess, kid?

KID

You're a dumb riddle.

GRIM REAPER

What's the matter? Scared of me?

KID

(Turns on light. Looks at boy beside the bed
in combat fatigues and leaning on a scythe.)

Not anymore, I'm not.

GRIM REAPER

Oh, no? Didn't I hear you moaning about not getting to grow up? Well, I'm Mr. Death. I don't believe we've met, have we? I had a visit with your great-grandmother, but you were only a toddler back then. Anyway, she died in her sleep. I'd been gone for hours before anyone noticed that I'd stopped by.

KID

You're just another kid.

GRIM REAPER

Want to see how I look to people that I've come to get?
(Holds up a grotesque rubber mask.)

KID

No!

GRIM REAPER

(Putting mask in pocket.)

Do you like my new combat fatigues? I wore out the old ones last week. It's been real busy out there.

KID
What's that big stick for?

GRIM REAPER
Swoosh! Swish! Mow 'em down like hay in a field! Like buttons and pencils and spoons, some things need no improvement.
(Swooshes and swishes around the room.)

KID
Quiet! I'm supposed to be asleep.

GRIM REAPER
(Leaning scythe against the dresser.)
My arms are tired anyway. That big trainwreck in Korea and the earthquake in Peru. Soon I'm going back to Africa for new epidemics of cholera and malaria. Boring diseases, but they keep me busy now that smallpox seems to be gone for good. And bubonic plague, you don't see that much these days. Legionnaires' disease and toxic shock, swine flu and Mad Cow disease—just lightweights compared to good old-fashioned Black Death. It put a third of Europe six feet under, that impressed even me. As for leprosy, good riddance, never cared for it. It goes on practically forever, and the corpses are all...
(Makes a disgusted face.)
Yuck. Anyway, who needs those nasty little bugs of Nature when your grown-ups build such wonderful weapons of war? Have you been watching the news lately? Wow!

KID
(Pulling the covers over his head.)
Go away.

GRIM REAPER
Hey, I hope I'm not depressing you. I stopped by to put your mind at ease about kicking the bucket. Take it from me, it's inevitable. You

know, breathing your last, laying down your burden, shuffling off this mortal coil.

> (Strolls about, slashing air with scythe.)

Giving up the ghost, meeting your Maker, cashing in your chips, and...

> (Pirouettes with scythe extended.)

...checking out, kicking off, and passing on. Not to mention my personal favorite—croaking.

> (Makes croaking noises in throat. Pauses,
> peeks under covers.)

Hey, you like jokes? How many photographers does it take to screw in a light bulb?

KID

You tell me.

GRIM REAPER

None, because they'd rather be in a darkroom!

> (Turns out the light and exits.)

SCENE 2

> (Same darkened bedroom. Window slides
> up. KID turns on light as GIRL climbs in.)

KID

This is too weird.

GIRL

Knock-knock.

KID

What is this, comedy night?

                    GIRL
No, I mean can I come in?

                    KID
How many people did you kill today?

                    GIRL
Oh, I'm not like *him*.

                    KID
Are you like me? I doubt it. Kids like me don't climb in other
people's windows in the middle of the night. Or transport down into
bedrooms from death stars. Maybe you're not like him, but you're
definitely not like me. Me, I stay in bed at night and try to sleep because I got school tomorrow. Pretty strange life, huh? Boring, right?

                    GIRL
                (Approaching bed.)
Hey, I knew you were a cool-looking kid, but wow, this is 3-D kinda
cool, you know? Rad pajamas! They got feetsies?
                (GIRL lifts covers to peek. KID yanks them back.)

                    KID
No, they don't have feetsies! I'm ten, not two!

                    GIRL
You don't have to act so get-away-from-me-ish. We're gonna get
married after college.

                    KID
Oh, no, I have a nightmare and who do I meet? The girl of my
dreams.

                    GIRL
No, the girl of your dreams dumped you in high school for some jock
who quoted Kurt Cobain. I'm the girl you married. You always
cheer me up when--

KID

Who's Kurt Cobain?

GIRL

…when I'm depressed, so I'm returning the favor so that you'll owe me later. Get it?—owe me later! Hey, where's your pet iguana?

KID

I don't have a pet iguana yet! Mom says I'm not old enough! And I probably never will be! You shoulda been here listening to Mr. Death! I hope you didn't let any mosquitos in—malaria is making a comeback. One little bite and… swoosh, there goes my head.

(GIRL giggles, covering her mouth.)

KID

Oh, warped! Maybe you should marry Mr. Death instead! Hang around the war zones together! Spend your honeymoon at a hospice!

GIRL

It just sounded funny. I'm sorry if I laughed.

KID

What do you mean, 'if you laughed?' You *did* laugh!

GIRL

Well, after you've been grown up you can laugh about things that scared you as a kid.

KID

That's easy for you to say, because you got to grow up. You don't have to worry about not getting to grow up once you've already done it. Me, I'm not just visiting here. I *am* here.

GIRL

But that's why I came back. So I could tell you that you are going to grow up. Doesn't that cheer you up a little?

51

KID

Oh, right.

(Puts a grin on his face, mugs the room.)

See how happy I am, everybody? You know why? I know I get to grow up. Guess how? My future wife came back to give me that important information.

(Shakes his head in disgust.)

Dummy! You've never heard of alternate realities? You've never read any stories about time-travel? There's lots of different futures, you know.

GIRL

Oh, like those science-fiction movies you always drag me to. Here's a clue. When you do grow up, don't assume your wife will be as fascinated by space aliens and imaginary worlds as you are, okay? As long as I'm back here not cheering you up, I may as well save myself major trauma later.

KID

Now I know you're from an alternate universe. I haven't even met you yet and already we're fighting. I'd have to be crazy to marry you!

GIRL

You are crazy! You don't improve with age, either, watch and see!

(They hear knocking at the bedroom door.)

KID

Great, you woke up the authority figures. Mom and Dad are going to kill me. Turns out I don't get to grow up after all.

GIRL

Sorry!

(Runs to window and climbs out.)

SCENE 3

(Same bedroom. Light is still on.)

DAD
(Sticking head into room.)

Son?

KID

Dad?

(Stares at youthful parents entering room.)
Oh, no. Not you guys, too.

MOM

We were sure we heard you talking to your future bride.

DAD

We thought we'd have a nice family chat, make hot chocolate with marshmallows...

MOM

I bet she's a sweet girl.

KID

Sweet like cyanide. She just went back out the window. If you guys hurry you might catch up with her. Keep a sharp eye out for Mr. Death—he's prowling the neighborhood, armed and dangerous.

DAD

Oh, is that what's keeping you awake?

KID

He's got a scythe as big as a flagpole, but he says with all the bombs he hardly needs it.

DAD

You know, son, things seemed pretty bleak when I was your age.

KID

You *are* my age.

(MOM sits on edge of bed. DAD paces.)

MOM

Your dad's telling you the truth. Both of us were worried about the world getting blown up. The US and the Soviet Union were in a terrible nuclear arms race.

KID

A race that's gotten pretty crowded.

MOM

But even the threat of thermonuclear war didn't stop other wars from happening. There was Korea and then Vietnam. Your uncle Mike fought over there. He still has nightmares about it.

DAD

Darling, please. He's just a kid.

KID

Which is probably how I'll be remembered.

MOM

And then we fought in Grenada for some reason I don't recall, and then in Panama, and then there was the first Gulf War. The second Gulf War will be coming up real soon. And...
(Turns to DAD.)
Didn't I leave one out, dear?

DAD

I think that's enough about war, darling.

MOM

Iraq and Afghanistan aren't too far off, either...

DAD

Darling...

MOM

But we don't have wars in this country. We're not some banana re-
public with military coups or wars of liberation or guerrilla rebels
hiding in the hills. Now that we have the nuclear bombs, all we ever
have is itty-bitty wars. And we fight them in other countries.

KID

That's a big comfort, Mom.

DAD

As I was saying, son, things were darned discouraging but everything
turned out fine. We grew up and got married and had you. What's
changed? Not much, really.

MOM

Well, some things. There's the weapons in schools. At a PTA meeting I heard one boy tried to stab another boy to steal his tennis shoes.

KID

I never heard about that.

MOM

Well, of course not, honey. The second boy pulled out a gun and shot
him.

DAD

Darling, I think that was in a different school.

MOM

That's right, it was. See, honey? You don't have to worry. Just be
careful. Like when you're riding your bike, watch out for all the

drunk drivers. And don't talk to strangers or get in cars with people you don't know or walk around alone at night. And everything will be fine.

                    DAD

The world is screwy, but statistically pretty near everybody gets to grow up.

                    MOM

Feel better now, honey?

                    (MOM leans down to kiss KID's forehead.)

                    KID

Stop it, Mom. Gross.

                    (DAD and MOM go to bedroom door.)

                    MOM

Now you know to call 911 if anything *should* happen?

                    KID

Right, Mom.

                    (As door closes, KID turns out light.)

Or Dial-a-Prayer.

SCENE 4

                    (Same dark bedroom. Bumping noises are
                    heard from closet. ALEXANDER and
                    MOZART can be heard arguing, off.)

                    ALEXANDER

Go on! March right out there!

MOZART

A march? Wouldn't a funeral dirge be more fitting?

ALEXANDER

That's all you ever think about! Music!

MOZART

Of course it has its limitations. It couldn't soothe your savage breast.

ALEXANDER

Who are you calling a savage? Listen, Greece had its Golden Age when you barbarians were gathering nuts and berries and wearing animal skins.

MOZART

But did you have composers?

ALEXANDER

In the name of Zeus, we had no need of concert halls! We had the lyre, didn't we? A fine instrument you likely never learned to play.

MOZART

That twangy soundbox made from a turtleshell?

ALEXANDER

And all the great philosophers were Greek. I myself studied under Aristotle.

MOZART

That imbecile who said that heavy things fall faster than light things?

ALEXANDER

He was right! They did, back then!

MOZART

And the world must have been smaller, too, for you to conquer it.

ALEXANDER

Out! Out, you pansy, you perfumed pianist!

> (KID turns on light. Shoving and grunting, two boys tumble from closet. ALEXANDER is clad in the battle gear of Ancient Greece. MOZART wears an embroidered waistcoat, knee-length pants with white stockings, powdered wig, and carries a rolled-up sheaf of music. They disengage and adjust their garb. KID eyes them.)

KID

Mom doesn't allow fighting in my room.

ALEXANDER

Fighting? Me, with him? I'll show you fighting.
> (Unsheaths his sword)

I'll cut out his heart, shrivelled prune that it is.

KID

Cut it out! No, don't cut it out!

ALEXANDER

Oh, you are a sorely confused young man, you are.

MOZART

Put that silly sword away, dear Alex. Swords don't frighten people in this day and age. These people are civilized. They have automatic weapons.

ALEXANDER

I should cut out your tongue instead of your heart. Never call me Alex. I am the Great Alexander, to you.

MOZART

Pooh.

(Extracts a dainty handkerchief and waves
it in the air.)

I surrender, your wondrous lordship. You're much too magnificent
for me.

KID

And who are you?

MOZART

You can call me Wolfie. I don't have *his* pretensions. I am a humble
musician.

ALEXANDER

Humble!

MOZART

I don't brag about composing operas when I was hardly twelve. Or
being appointed concertmaster at fifteen. Or touring the great capitals
of Europe to entertain kings and queens before I was twenty. Never,
not once.

(Sniffs a pinch from a snuffbox.)

ALEXANDER

Nor do I brag of leading the mightiest army on earth while still a boy!
Nor do I brag of subduing all of Asia Minor by the time I was thirty!
Nor of being the only great general in all history who was never de-
feated!

MOZART

Did I mention that I have perfect pitch? And that I have never forgotten a single note of a single piece of music I ever heard played?
That I composed symphonies in my sleep and wrote them down at
breakfast?

ALEXANDER

I died two years younger than you but I'm just as famous. Even
more!

59

MOZART
Ah, but the masses still love my music, while your empire is dust.
(Turns to KID)
Show him, dear child. Hum a bit of my piano concerto in B flat.

ALEXANDER
No! Tell this pathetic minstrel the name of my famous warhorse!

MOZART
Or my Requiem!

ALEXANDER
The legend of how I undid the Gordian knot!

MOZART
(Waving his sheaf of music.)
The names of my renowned operas!

ALEXANDER
The name of the great city I founded!

KID
I don't know anything! I'm in fifth grade!
(Climbs from bed and opens closet door.)
I don't know the answers for your stupid questions, so just go back through your time tunnel and let me sleep! How am I going to stay awake in math class?

MOZART
(To ALEXANDER)
Look how you've upset him. Befriend him, indeed. I should have come with James Dean. Or maybe Anastasia or Joan of Arc or Pocahontas. One of those charming young ladies snuffed out in early prime.

ALEXANDER
You always preferred the company of women, you whistling sissy.

KID

Hold on. You mean there's more of you in there?
(Peers into closet.)

MOZART

Dear child, surely you don't suppose we're the only two people who became famous and died before we grew up?

KID

But you *were* grown up!

MOZART

Hardly. Alexander here never knew a grey hair. And I—oh, what wonderful works I had yet to compose! Now all I can do is decompose.

ALEXANDER

You notice that he's not remembered for his wit.

MOZART

I'm sure nobody's forgotten your drunken temper, you insensitive bore!

ALEXANDER

Insensitive? I was a wise and learned ruler who tried to bring order to the world! And I would have accomplished it if Death hadn't interfered with my plans!

MOZART

Oh, as if Death didn't interfere with mine!

ALEXANDER

The unfairness of it!

MOZART

The brutality!

ALEXANDER

The injustice!

MOZART

The banality!

ALEXANDER

If I could only meet him face to face!

MOZART

We could repay him together!

KID

You want to find Mr. Death, is that it?

ALEXANDER

That schemer!

MOZART

That scoundrel!

KID

He was here a few minutes ago.

ALEXANDER

Where did he go? Tell us, and we'll put an end to your worries about dying!

MOZART

No children will ever worry again about the grim reaper!

KID

He went right into that closet, the same one you came out of.

ALEXANDER

After him!

(ALEXANDER and MOZART charge into closet. KID slams door behind them, then jumps into bed and reaches for light.)

KID

Finally!

SCENE 5

(Same bedroom. The bed is jostled as muttering can be heard from under it. KID sits up.)

KID

I can't stand this anymore! Now who's here?

MAN

You.

KID

You who?

MAN

No thanks.

KID

No thanks, what?

MAN

To a Yoo-Hoo. I never liked them. Aunt Mary used to insist I drink one. Wouldn't take no for an answer. Remember?

KID

I remember when Aunt Mary used to insist *I* drink one.

MAN

That's what I said.

KID

That's what *I* said.

MAN

Same difference.

> (Emerges from under the bed, boy-sized but
> very old and bent over, with a cane.)

KID

Who are you, Grandfather Time? Can't you guys leave me alone?

MAN

You are alone.

KID

Just me!

MAN

And this is just me.

KID

Just me me!

MAN

Mimi? Oh, what a woman! What a week in Paris that was! But you wouldn't remember her yet. Well, soon enough. Time flies. Which brings me to my point…

> (Beat.)

No, I lost it again.

KID

Can you stop your senior moment long enough to tell me who you are and why you're here? So far tonight, I've had Mr. Death—actually more like Kid Death—showing me the scythe he's going to cut me down with. Then my future wife tells me not to worry, because I live long enough to marry her. Then Alexander the Great and Mozart explain that dying young isn't such a bad thing, lots of famous people do it. How am I supposed to get any sleep? Doesn't anybody understand I have school tomorrow?

                    MAN
I thought you couldn't sleep. That's what everyone thought.

                    KID
I bet I can now. I'm sure tired of people traipsing in and out.

                    MAN
So you want me to leave?

                    KID
Yes!

                         (MAN shrugs, lays cane on bed and slowly
                         lowers himself to crawl under bed.)

                    KID
Hey, hold on.

                    MAN
Make up your mind. I'm ninety-three years old. This isn't so easy anymore.

                    KID
Before you go, who are you? Or who were you?

                    MAN
Well, I *was* you. But I forgot what an impatient young man I was.
                    (Stands up with effort.)
What's a little lost sleep? If Alexander the Great stopped by to chat with me, I'd talk to him all night. Same with Mozart. I'll bet they could tell you some stories! Hand me that cane.

KID
(Giving him the cane.)
I didn't think anybody used canes anymore.

MAN
Well, I have a motorized walker. But how was I supposed to bring it from under a bed?

KID
Oh, right. You have a motorized walker under there. Parked next to your flying saucer?

MAN
I'd forgotten what a smart-aleck kid I was. Precocious is not always a good thing.

KID
Okay, I get it. You're supposed to be me when I'm old. That's supposed to cure my worries about dying. Well, you're no more help than my future wife was. I guess you don't know about alternate universes, either. How there's a fork in the road whenever something happens, and depending on which direction you take you go into a different universe. Well, who's to say I take the same forks in the road as you did? I might take some different way. So maybe you've lived a long time, but it doesn't mean I will. I might end up in some universe where I don't get any older. Maybe tomorrow I'll get run over by a bus because I didn't put on clean socks in the morning.

MAN
I know all about alternate universes. I learned about them at the same time you did. We read the same science fiction stories, you know. But I've thought about the problem longer than you have.
(Pulls out desk chair and sits very slowly.)

KID
Yeah. Eighty-three years longer. Wow, you're old. Can you even touch your toes?

MAN

Can you grow a beard?

KID

Why would I want to grow a beard?

MAN

Why would I want to touch my toes?

KID

Oh, why don't you go back to your own universe. This is a stupid conversation.

MAN

You want a smarter one? Tell me, when a person gets to a fork in the road and can go into different universes, what determines which way he goes?

KID

He goes both ways! That's the whole point. Who you are splits into two different you's.

MAN

But what decides which one you feel like you are?

KID

(Makes a face.)

I guess whichever way I decide to go, that's the one I feel like I am.

MAN

Suppose you're about to step into the street when along comes a bus. You could call that a fork in the road, because something's going to happen: either you'll step out in front of the bus or you won't. If you don't, then you find yourself in a universe where the bus didn't run you over. Right? The other you *does* step into the street and *does* get hit by the bus and dies. But since you aren't him, you're still alive and well. There's the answer to your problem.

KID

What, don't step in front of buses and I'll live to be ninety-three?

MAN

Why not? You have free will.

KID

But things happen! Bad things happen!

MAN

Listen to me. Life isn't something that just happens. Life is something you make up as you go along. Take charge! When you make decisions, make them so you go into universes you want to be aware of being in. I know you can do it, because I did it, and I'm you.

KID

So you say. How is that, anyway? Have they invented time travel in the future?

MAN

I wish. If they had, I wouldn't be here gabbing with you. I'd be back in Paris with Mimi.

KID

Well, if there's no time travel, how'd you get here?

MAN

Oh, I'm not really here. I'm there in the future. I'm just remembering what it was like to be ten. You're a memory.

KID

Great. I'm only ten and nothing but a memory.
(Covers his face with a pillow.)

MAN

You're real in your time. It's in my time that you're a memory.

KID

I don't have any memory of you. So how come you're here big as
life in my time?

MAN

Wait! That's it! What I wanted to tell you! It was… It was…

KID

Oh, criminy.

(Tosses pillow.)

MAN

No, no, I've got it. *Imagination.*

KID

Imagination? Whose imagination? Mine or yours?

MAN

Both. People always used to tell me I had too much imagination.
That means you do, too.

KID

And that's it? That's supposed to help me sleep?

MAN

I've got an idea. Turn out the light. Let's get Mr. Death back in here.

KID

Why? He'll probably cut off my head with that scythe.

MAN

He won't.

KID

How do you know? Oh, yeahhhh, if he did that, he'd have already
done that, and you wouldn't be here. Got it.

(Turns off light.)

GRIM REAPER

Swish! Swish! Swish!

(KID turns light on.)

GRIM REAPER

What do you want me for? Are you ready to croak?

KID

Were you doing something more important?

GRIM REAPER

I was practicing.

KID

It doesn't seem to me you need practice. How many people died to-day?

GRIM REAPER

(Gazes up as he does mental calculations.)

 A million, more or less. It's been slow. There's a cease-fire in the Middle East.

(Pointing at MAN.)

Who's your decrepit friend?

KID

That's me eighty-three years from now.

GRIM REAPER

Huh. He's old. How'd I miss him?

MAN

I've been dodging you for years.

GRIM REAPER

Well, you can't keep it up forever.

                    MAN

One day at a time.

                    (Nudges KID.)

Here's how you take charge. Get out of bed and take that scythe
away from him.

                    GRIM REAPER

What? Don't even try it.

                    MAN

Go on. I dare you.

                    KID

You think I can?

                    MAN

I know you can.

                    (KID climbs from bed, goes to GRIM
                    REAPER, snatches scythe away.)

                    GRIM REAPER

Hey, that's not fair! Give me back my scythe!

                    (Grabs for scythe but KID keeps it away.)

You're going to have an overpopulation problem if you don't let me
have that!

                    MAN

See? He's just in your imagination.

                    GRIM REAPER

I'm real!

                    (Stamping his foot.)

I'm as real as you are! Give me that thing and I'll show you how real
I am!

(Closet door opens. ALEXANDER and
MOZART emerge.)

ALEXANDER
(Brandishes his sword.)
Aha! We meet again! Where's your sting now, you sneak-in-the-
night, you rotten double-crosser! I never got to conquer China because of you!

GRIM REAPER
You didn't even know there was a China!
(Dancing away from sword thrusts.)
Not fair! Not fair! You've got a sword!

ALEXANDER
Death, prepare to die!

GRIM REAPER
(Dodging sword swings.)
After all the help I gave you and your armies? All the times we
marched together? This is how you show your gratitude?

MOZART
Let me do it! Do you know how many concertos I still wanted to
write?
(Grabs GRIM REAPER from behind and
starts hitting him with sheaf of music.)

GRIM REAPER
Get away from me, you... you corpses! I let you both get famous
first, didn't I? I ought to kill you all over again, that's what I ought
to do! Give me my scythe!

(Window opens. GIRL tumbles in. She
runs to KID as he is chased by GRIM
REAPER, who is chased by ALEXANDER
and MOZART.)
72

GIRL

Leave my husband alone, you monster!

> (GIRL begins slapping GRIM REAPER in
> the chest while ALEXANDER   tries to
> get a sword swing and MOZART smacks
> GRIM REAPER in the head with sheaf of
> music.)

KID

(To MAN)

Wow, she's got a temper. I'm supposed to marry her? I don't think so!

MAN

When the time comes, you'll change your mind.

> (Bedroom door opens. DAD and MOM
> look on in astonishment.)

DAD

What on earth is going on in here! We're trying to watch the Tonight Show.

MOM

Sweetie, it's a school night. No parties on school nights, you know the rule.

GRIM REAPER

Make him give me back my scythe!

MOM

Give the man his scythe, Sweetie. That thing looks awfully sharp.

GIRL

(To KID.)

Oh, introduce me to your parents, please, please?

(KID slaps himself on the forehead, grabs sleeve of MAN as MAN crawls under the bed.)

KID

Where do you think you're going? What am I supposed to do about all this?

MAN

Use your imagination, kid.

(As MAN disappears, GIRL pulls KID toward MOM and DAD.)

KID
(With exasperation.)
Mom, Dad? This is the girl I'm going to marry.

MOM

Oh, isn't that sweet? What's her name?

KID

I don't know yet.

DAD

Don't you think you ought to find that out, son?

(MOM embraces GIRL, then KID. KID hands scythe to GIRL, who hands it to Dad, who hands it to GRIM REAPER as he runs past while pursued by ALEXANDER and MOZART.)

GRIM REAPER
(Whirling and brandishing scythe.)
Say your prayers, fellas!

KID

Oh, no, here we go again.

>(GRIM REAPER squares off against AL-
>EXANDER and they battle around room
>with scythe against sword.)

MOM

Oh, goodness.

>(MOM follows them, picking up everything
>they knock over.)

MOZART

>(To GIRL with a deep bow)

Why, hello there. Aren't you a portrait of perfection?

GIRL

Thank you. You're quite handsome yourself.

MOZART

Be still my heart! Are you wed?

GIRL

I'm engaged to be married.

MOZART

Has anyone ever composed a concerto for you? It'll only take a
minute. Is there a piano in the house?

DAD

>(Following KID as he searches under bed.)

Son, we need to have a talk about your sleep schedule.

ALEXANDER

>(To MOZART, while dodging scythe.)

Charge his flank, Wolfie!

MOZART

Not now! This angel is inspiring me!

ALEXANDER

Wolfie! You're two hundred years older than she is!

DAD
(Tapping GRIM REAPER on shoulder.)
Look, can you put down that scythe before someone loses an eye?

GRIM REAPER
(To DAD, while defending against sword.)
Say, how old are you? Do you smoke? How's your cholesterol?
(Dodges as sword knocks books off desk.)

MOM
(To ALEXANDER)
Young man, give me that sword!

(MOZART kisses GIRL's hand.)

GIRL

Ewww!

(She pulls free and hurries away.)

MOZART
(Pursuing GIRL)
My little rosebud, come back! You can be my muse!

DAD
(Pursuing MOZART)
Hey there, you! That's my daughter-in-law!

GRIM REAPER
(Pursuing DAD)
How's the old ticker, buddy? Mind if I check your blood pressure?

(Pulls out a blood pressure cuff and tries to strap it on DAD's arm.)

ALEXANDER
(Pursuing GRIM REAPER)
Death, you coward, face me like a man!

MOM
(Pursuing ALEXANDER)
Give me that sword or I'll have to call your parents!

(GIRL in forefront of chase runs into KID's arms. The others crash together behind her. Melee ensues with shoves and grunts.)

KID
(Jumping onto bed.)
Stop it! Everybody stop!
(He waits for everyone's attention.)
I've decided I won't worry anymore about not getting to grow up. Instead of that I'm going to think about what I want to do when I *am* a grown-up. So I won't need any of you around. You can leave.

(VISITORS look about, bewildered.)

KID
Go back where you came from! Now!

(ALEXANDER and MOZART, grumbling and elbowing, go into closet. MOM and DAD, shaking heads, go out bedroom door. GIRL with reluctance goes out window.)

MAN
(Sticking head out from under bed.)
Attaboy. Couldn't've said it better myself.

                    KID
                    (Pointing forefinger.)
You, too. Back to the future.

                            (MAN scoots under bed. KID circles room,
                            closing window and doors. Turns to find
                            GRIM REAPER in middle of room.)

                    GRIM REAPER
That's better. I get enough craziness on the job. It gets tiresome.

                    KID
You, too. Go find a shipwreck or something.

                    GRIM REAPER
Me?

                    KID
You especially.

                    GRIM REAPER
Couldn't we play cards for a while?

                    KID
Out!

                    GRIM REAPER
Shoot some dice? Talk philosophy?

                    KID
                    (Climbs into bed, turns off light. After
                    pause, turns light back on. GRIM REA-
                    PER is gone. Turns light off again and
                    yawns.)
What a night!

(After a long pause KID begins snoring.
Footsteps pitter-patter onto stage. Lights
come up enough to see all KID's visitors
sneak back on tiptoes. They make a semi-
circle around the bed, gazing down at KID,
smiling and nudging each other. They turn
toward audience.)

VISITORS
(With fingers to lips.)

Shhhhh…

(They crouch with heads bowed. Curtain.)

The Plutonium Kid

The official story is that the Plutonium Kid is dead. He died from a congenital heart defect this last October thirtieth outside the Mark Hopkins Hotel in San Francisco. But official stories are always deceptive in one way or another, by definition. If they were wholly true they would need no stamp of officialdom to establish their veracity. So it is with this story. In an unofficial version of the story, the Plutonium Kid did not die. He never had a congenital heart defect, and although he was on California Street last October thirtieth, neither of the two unfortunate deaths occurring at that time was his.

How he came to be there on that day and why an official story was concocted to account for his disappearance from public view is a tale in itself and not a pretty one. It could never be given a stamp of officialdom, because it nakedly exposes the consequences of the monstrous greed and breathtaking arrogance of modern times. It does fit the facts in evidence, however, and its saving grace, as with most unofficial stories, is that it constitutes a love story.

This unofficial story begins not with the birth of the Plutonium Kid, but with his being found as an infant by Henry and Marie le Strange. Graduate students from Berkeley, the young couple was hiking on Mt. Tamalpais that summer morning. Mt. Tam is a coastal peak just north of San Francisco, and Henry had veered off the trail for a view of the city of Mill Valley nestled below. He nearly stumbled over the infant lying in a cluster of California poppies. It basked happily in the warm sunshine, pumping its arms and legs in its blissful solitude.

"I've found someone's baby," Henri called.

While Henri waited for Marie, he wondered if perhaps the parents might have placed it there while somewhere nearby they went about conceiving a sibling for the boy. Certainly no parent could have left it accidentally in such an unusual location.

"Oh, I do so love Mt. Tam!" was Marie's reaction. "Every time I come here I see something new!" And she gathered the baby into her generous embrace.

A cheerfully plump art major at Berkeley, Marie had never had a real boyfriend until she met and immediately slept with and the next day married the young physicist Henri le Strange, who was visiting from France. She didn't care that it was the imminent expiration of Henri's student visa that motivated his proposal, because she didn't expect to stay with him forever. They made excellent companions, both of them accommodating and affectionate, and made love every night. It is fair to say that they shared more happiness than any other couple in their collegiate circle, in no small part because neither of them cared what might befall their relationship in the long-term.

Perhaps they weren't the right couple to find the infant. They didn't intend to have children, not even their own. What they did was carefully transport the baby down the mountainside and hand it over to a woman from Child Protective Service. While the woman filled out paperwork, Marie cradled it in her arms and cooed, "Little guy, don't you worry about a thing." Forms were filled out, as forms must be, and the infant entered the system with the name Guy le Strange.

*

The "le" of the name was converted to the middle initial "L" when the baby arrived at the St. Catherine orphanage in Santa Rosa. Before long the L came to stand for "Little," with the nuns referring to him as "Strange Little Guy." Other children at the orphanage, who usually paid no attention to newborns, frequently lurked by the nursery to spy on the newborn they tagged with the nickname "Strangeguy."

In appearance and nature he indeed became a strange little guy. His frame was loose-limbed and lean and his face matured into an isoceles triangle with the tip pointed down. He had wide-set blue eyes that expressed an active intelligence and somewhat compensated for the fact that he never spoke. He avoided social interactions, preferring instead to watch television programs on wildlife. Occasionally the other boys coaxed him into games that involved dice and he excelled at them, but he refused to participate in roughhousing or physical sports.

Such peculiarities fell within the normal range of behaviors for boys. There was a significant aspect, however, that validated his surname. His teeth could not be x-rayed.

"Bite down on this and hold very still," the dental hygenist told him, before slipping into the hallway and pressing the button that would shoot high-frequency electromagnetic rays through his baby teeth.

No image appeared on the negative. No image appeared when she tried again, and her third and fourth tries also proved unsuccessful. The hygienist was not bewildered, because she knew that the internal x-ray tube had to be replaced occasionally. Until the new part arrived, however, no more x-rays could be taken. Six children with appointments trooped back to the minivan and Sister Veronica drove them back to the orphanage.

The following Monday they returned. Guy went last of the six. Before long he trudged back into the waiting room with the dentist behind him.

"The new x-ray tube burned out," he told Sister Veronica. "But my visual examination of this fellow doesn't show any problems." He patted Guy's curly blond head and chuckled, "When the tech comes out maybe I should have him look at this boy instead of the machine."

Six months later it happened again, and the dentist abandoned his sense of humor.

"The boy is jinxed," he informed Sister Veronica. "I can't x-ray him, and if I can't x-ray him I can't have him as a patient."

There is an effective gossip grapevine in the obsessive-compulsive world of dentists. When Sister Veronica shopped for a new dentist she was turned down everywhere. She finally settled for having a dental hygienist visit the orphanage twice a year to clean Guy's teeth, which luckily were immune to dental caries.

*

"One more thing," Sister Veronica told the corpulent visitor in a shabby suit who professed to be looking for a son to adopt. "Little Guy exhibits Asperger's Syndrome. You are familiar with the syndrome?"

"Not life-threatening, is it?" The man's grey-black eyebrows merged in a frown.

"No, not life-threatening."

"And not contagious?"

"No, not contagious. It's like a milder version of autism."

"Autism, of course. No problem at all. I had a sister with autism and an aunt on my father's side, the both of them suffered with autism."

"Then you know how emotionally taxing it can be for a parent."

The man vigorously nodded. "He's been clinically tested, I take it? No armchair diagnostics here? No, no, of course not."

Sister Veronica drew herself up. "We at St. Catherine's are accustomed to a wide range of maladaptive behaviors. When I tell you Guy is autistic, I don't mean stand-offish. I mean that he can't tolerate very much sensory stimulation unless he has control over it. You see how he keeps the television remote in his lap?"

The man was nodding in full agreement before she finished. "Oh, he'd have his own remote, most certainly."

"And don't be deceived into thinking that he'd be an affectionate boy. Hugs and kisses, that sort of feedback that parents expect from their children. Little Guy never cared much for being touched. Now that he's sixteen he likes it even less."

"Of course not," the man said, shaking his large head decisively. "No kisses and hugs. Not even on birthdays."

They both looked across the recreation room at the blond boy who intently watched as a lion devoured a wildebeest on the television screen.

Sudden worry appeared on the visitor's face. "He can be talked to?"

"Yes, but loud male voices can be distressing for him. He responds best to a woman's voice, especially if it's soothing. You're married, I assume."

"No, no, not married." The man hurriedly amended this reply. "About to be. Married, that is. Oh, yes, wonderful woman. Loves kids, loves them." His large head nodded vigorously.

"No one has ever asked to adopt little Guy," said the nun. "He's very hard to reach."

"This is the one. I'm sure of it."

"It's a lengthy process. There are quite a few hoops to jump through."

"My attorney does my jumping," the man said benignly. He patted a belly that stretched the seams of his plaid vest. "Robert Kroeker, good man. Waiting outside."

Sister Veronica's flinty eyes flicked protectively in Guy's direction.

"Ordinarily these decisions are not made so precipitously, Mr... Sorry, how is it pronounced again?"

"Malikovsky. Sergei Malikovsky. And introduce me to the boy, would you, Sister? It's time he met his new father, I think."

*

There was a perfectly blue sky on the day Guy left the orphanage. Kroeker drove. Guy rode in the back seat with his adoptive father. In air-conditioned silence they rode across the Golden Gate Bridge and into the bright fantasia of San Francisco. At the top of Nob Hill they parked in the entrance drive of the Mark Hopkins hotel. Cable cars clacked and screeched on both streets of the intersection, people laden with cameras and shopping bags getting on and off. The hotel valet approached to take the car.

Sergei Malikovsky grunted as he maneuvered his corpulence out of the back seat. Grasping Guy's wrist, he tugged him out. Together they ascended the curved marble steps. Malikovsky leaned down confidentially.

"Your new home," he said. "It's a famous hotel. If you like it, I may even buy it for you."

*

Cherie Pei strolled from her bedroom in the luxurious Terrace Suite of the Mark Hopkins Hotel to meet her newly-adopted son. The faint swishing of her red Chinese pajamas hung in her wake like an aural perfume. Her smile was as radiant as the morning sunrise. She took Guy's hands smoothly in hers and released them before he had a chance to react.

Her first words to him were cautionary.

"Since I am to be your new mother, it would be inappropriate for you to fall in love with me. So don't do it. Now give me a big hug."

It was an absurd warning, but Cherie knew that. Men of all ages and types fell in love with her, and who could blame them? She had inherited chiselled cheekbones and long legs from her Russian grandmother, full lips and almond eyes from her Chinese father, and stunning curves from her Swedish mother. When first introduced to Cherie, men were struck dumb with wonder. She smiled and wonder escalated to lust. She spoke and lust turned into idolatry. This had become such a familiar phenomenon in Cherie's life that she took it for granted. Objects fell to the floor when she dropped them, too. It was a fact of life.

Her arms enfolded him. She hugged until she was sure he knew her breasts were naked inside her silk pajamas. Stepping back, she caressed his shoulders.

"I will always be near when you need me," she assured him, "and will never bother you when you want to be alone. We are going to be best friends."

And she leaned forward and bestowed a kiss on his flushed cheek.

*

"How did it go?" Malikovsky asked.

"Oh, he's already in love with me."

"Spooky little bastard, isn't he?"

"He looks like a space alien," Cherie said.

86

"He looks like a money machine," Malikovsky said. "And am I ever wrong about those?"

The question was rhetorical so Cherie didn't bother answering. She, after all, was another of Sergei Malikovsky's money machines. Cherie's extraordinary appearance had earned her a self-indulgent life since she turned thirteen and fled her last foster home, but it had been on the arms of con men who ended up in prison sooner or later. Sergei had won her from the last crook in a game of poker. The brokenhearted man had hanged himself afterward, and Sergei had secured his hold on her heart by somberly escorting her to the funeral. Cherie had been invaluable ever since, because many men resistant to bribes will wade gladly into a swamp of corruption for the attentions of a seductive woman.

And Cherie had witnessed a global panorama of corruption. There was literally nothing that men wouldn't sell out. For a price as banal as an envelope of money a politician would sell out millions of constituents. For the promise of a generous retirement a bureaucrat would give up a nation's critical secrets. For a junket to little-girl brothels of Bangkok a law enforcement official would turn a blind eye to rampant racketeering.

In her eight years with Sergei, Cherie had seen it all. She had seen Sergei arrange exchanges of defense technology for illegal campaign contributions. She had seen him promise billions in foreign aid for the right to lay an oil pipeline. She had seen him trade encryption software for a Security Council vote.

Cherie had played a key role in these deals. She acted as both temptation and prize. Cherie intuitively understood a man's dark secrets and how to become the personification of his desire. This she had learned about men in authority: they might be charismatic and crafty, demagogic and dangerous, mealy-mouthed and mendacious, but deep inside they were always weak. They sought and gained their power for a shield to protect them when they gave in to their weakness. And when they gave in, they always betrayed their office. It was like a law of society, that the men chosen to lead it were the men most likely to befoul it.

Such men had groped her in corporate offices, had made her kneel in limousines, had laid her on her back in staterooms, and she no longer believed that such men ran the world. It was plain to her that their leadership was a sham. Their weakness could be exploited by cleverer men and always was. She had come to believe that nationalism itself was an illusion, that the institutions of government were no more than a Potemkin village built to provide a sense of continuity and stability for the common people.

When she suggested this stark observation to Sergei he shrugged his heavy shoulders. They were sprawled on the bed in post-coital languor, having earlier arranged a difficult deal in which France had agreed to increase its quota of Arab immigrants in exchange for cessation of terrorist attacks.

"History wants to move along at its own speed," Malikovsky told her. "Tick-tick-tick, like a clock. It doesn't want to stop. But governments and corporations and churches, they try to slow it down or stop it. So that things stay the way they are. What everyone everywhere wants is for everything to stand still. If things stand still, what is good will stay good. If things aren't good, at least they won't get any worse."

He reached for the bottle of champagne and poured two flutes full. He handed one to Cherie and clinked his against it.

"You and I fight on the side of time and history, which must always go forward. We fight on the side of nature. We help things change, like they are supposed to. Do you know the story of the Rosenbergs? They were husband and wife in New York City. After World War Two, they handed over the secret of the atom bomb to the Russians. America put them on trial for spying, executed them. Why? Because Americans wanted to keep the atom bomb just for themselves. Americans wanted to control the earth. They wanted to be able to drop atom bombs on anyone who resisted. They wanted history to stand still for them. But the Rosenbergs were on the side of time and history, like us. Sadly, they were idealists and idealists are fools. History despises idealists. It squashes them like bugs. History doesn't like owing favors. It pays its debts on the spot and it pays with cash. That is why fools like the Rosenbergs rot in their graves while you and I drink five hundred dollar champagne in a famous hotel and keep fortunes in our bank accounts."

Cherie snuggled against his brawny chest and thought for a while about what he said.

"Sergei," she asked, "do you think someday we'll have a child of our own?"

"I already have seventeen," he grunted. "They are seventeen headaches."

"But I have none."

"You have this one," Sergei said. "Don't be so foolish to ask for more."

*

An x-ray tube was concealed overnight in Guy's room. It functioned perfectly the following morning. Malikovsky was incensed.

"What happened to him wasn't just coincidence!" he shouted at Cherie. "Stupid little bimbo, what do you know about the smell of money? The little boy reeks of it!" He spun his corpulent body toward his attorney. "Explain this to me, Kroeker!"

"Maybe it only happens when the tube is turned on," Kroeker said.

The next day Kroeker introduced to them an assistant researcher from Stanford. They all sat around the glass-topped table on the terrace. Guy had been entrusted to a personal trainer at the hotel fitness center across the street.

The nuclear researcher methodically counted through the thick stack of hundred dollar bills. When satisfied he stashed them in a fanny pack and opened his knapsack.

"Here are three self-luminous materials," he said, lining up glass jars on the table. "They can be handled safely. But I also brought samples of cobalt 60 and uranium 238." He carefully took two cylindrical lead containers from the backpack. "They're seriously radioactive, so when you finish with them, be sure you dispose of them properly. Or drop them in the Pacific."

"Which ones give off x-rays?" Malikovsky asked.

"The cobalt emits gamma and beta. The uranium gives off alpha."

"We asked for x-rays," Malikovsky said with narrowed eyes.

"Gamma rays are high-frequency photons. Same thing."

"But alpha and beta aren't x-rays, are they?" Malikovsky said. "Why should I pay for them?"

"You wanted radiation-emitting materials, right? Alpha and beta particles are radiation, too. But they're actual particles, not photons. And trust me, they'll kill you just as dead."

He held out a small Geiger counter.

"This I threw in for free. Just turn it on and listen for the clicking." He unscrewed the cap on one of the lead containers and switched the detector on. It clicked at a furious rate, and he closed the container again. With a cloth napkin he deftly wiped everything clean of fingerprints.

He shouldered his knapsack and left the suite. He didn't even give Cherie a last look.

*

There was nothing discouraging about tests this time. What was truly extraordinary was the effect that Guy had on the cobalt and uranium. While he was still at the fitness center, those made the Geiger counter click rapidly each time they tested it. But as Cherie returned to the hotel with Guy, the device went completely silent.

"Can it be true?" Malikovsky marvelled. "Can it be true?"

Kroeker proposed that they try a different Geiger counter. It was an hour before he came back with a top-of-the-line model. It was silent as well.

For a few moments the three of them were still. Then Malikovsky began to grin. He grinned and began to bellow with laughter. He danced like an ungainly bear. He grabbed Cherie by the arm and twirled her. Even the reserved Kroeker danced, stamping his feet while he waved arms erratically and hooted.

They had activated the money machine.

*

Cherie considered the task she had been assigned while watching Sergei hum to himself as he got dressed. Sergei stood six foot two and a half inches tall and he weighed three hundred eleven pounds, but apart from his great bulk he managed an unimpressive appearance. He wore a baggy brown suit with a wrinkled rayon tie and always the same loafers on his short wide feet. He did nothing to disguise his sagging jowls, and his greying hair seemed overdue for a haircut even as he walked out of the barbershop. At a first glance he could be thought the proprietor of an adult book store or a cheapskate slumlord. Neither his carriage nor his mannerisms contradicted such a first impression. Sergei concealed his ruthlessness and genius behind an orchestrated image of ordinariness. He allowed others to perceive his true nature only when it served his purposes.

His willingness and ability to perpetuate this deceit frightened Cherie more than his temper did. She could cope with incendiary outbursts and was no stranger to violence, but the strength of will necessary for a billionaire to pretend himself a buffoon seemed to her proof of demonic inhabitation. Sergei was a man more powerful than presidents, premiers and princes, because he could accomplish anything and answered to nobody, yet he preferred that commoners think him harmless. He manipulated the cultivated illusion and the underlying reality with such skill that it took only the slightest change of expression for the former to be replaced by the latter.

Whenever Cherie saw this happen and saw the shock writ large on the face of the unfortunate recipient, a terrible thrill gripped her. It couldn't be dispelled until Sergei possessed her again in his usual aggressive fashion. Cherie knew this thrill wasn't real love, but it was very similar and as close to love as she wanted to get. Unlike love, it was episodic, which in Cherie's mind made it superior. In between these occasional terrible thrills, she thought of herself as Sergei's highly-trained operative and engaged in her seductive duties without emotion. While not contemptuous of her spineless victims, Cherie felt no qualms as she robbed them of every shred of integrity and debauched their virtue before giving them a perfunctory kiss goodbye.

However, Guy presented something of a problem. He was soon to be her legal son, so he had to be handled with care. The court already took a dim view of Malikovsky's adoption as a single parent. In California adoption required a six month trial period, and the judge had made clear to Sergei that final approval was conditional on Cherie and Sergei being married by then. Any hint of impropriety would cause revocation of that agreement.

The larger issue was that Guy was an innocent. Cherie had little experience with innocence. She could barely recall her own. Nor did Guy have integrity to steal. It dawned on Cherie that not until a man lost his innocence could he possess integrity. Integrity was what a man created to replace the innocence he had lost.

Cherie decided that since Guy didn't possess integrity she would have to steal his innocence.

By his response to their first hug she felt she understood him and she proceeded with confidence. She took advantage of the summer weather that had arrived in the city and began sunbathing on the terrace of the suite. It was furnished with a chaise lounge that folded out flat, and Cherie was lying face-down on the chaise wearing nothing but her bikini bottoms when Guy padded into the living room.

She called and he came out, blinking in the brightness, clad in the denim shorts and polo shirt she had bought him at Abercrombie and Fitch.

"Darling," she said, "would you rub some sunblock lotion on my shoulders?"

Without a word Guy knelt beside the chaise lounge. He squeezed a dollop from the tube and thoughtfully warmed it in his palms before slathering it on her skin.

"Oh, you've done this before," Cherie purred. "For your girlfriends?"

Guy shook his head slowly.

"No girlfriend ever?

Again Guy shook his head. His face remained stoic.

"Well, the one you never had doesn't know what she's missing."

Cherie found the stroking and rolling of his fingertips disconcertingly pleasurable. More than merely rubbing the sunblock in, he was massaging along her spine and doing it deftly. When he kneaded her shoulders she sighed dreamily. She drifted into a familiar fantasy about the Riviera. Two summers previous she had been assigned by Sergei to flirt with a fat diplomat there. But in her fantasy the diplomat became a Grand Prix racer married to her imaginary prim sister. Lulled by the magic of his adulterous hands, Cherie fell into sleep.

She awoke to hands playing with her honey-golden hair. Drowsily she rolled onto her side. She felt the hot sun on her full nude breasts at the same moment she saw Guy's pale blue eyes widen.

"Oh!" She crossed her tawny arms over her bare torso with real embarrassment. "Now get along. I'll do my front by myself."

When she heard him rummaging in the kitchenette, she sat erect, straddling the chaise. She took a moment to clear her head. This is an assignment, she told herself. You know how to do this. Guy's padding footsteps entered the living room again and stopped. Cherie took a deep breath and uncrossed her arms and squeezed out lotion. She began oiling her breasts in a circular fashion, spiralling toward the mounded nipples and giving them particular attention. Lying back on the chaise, she closed her eyes against the bright summer sun and wondered for how long he would stare at the splendid view she provided.

*

"I estimate the boy's range to be twenty yards," Kroeker said. It was late in the day, and he dropped wearily into a chair by the window. Malikovsky paced and Cherie perched on the foot of the bed. "But it's a guess."

"I don't pay you for guesses," Malikovsky growled.

He had called this informal conference upon their return from the hospital. An administrator there had escorted him and Kroeker to the secure basement where radioactive medical waste was stored. There were two lead-lined lockers on wheels—the larger for low-level waste, the smaller for intermediate-level. Both displayed yellow and black emblems to signify radiation. Kroeker opened and tested them with the Geiger counter.

"Contaminated clothing and gloves and so on," the administrator said with the larger locker. With the smaller he said, "Radiating devices, mostly. In nuclear medicine we use cesium, cobalt, iridium, strontium, and iodine. They have short half-lives, so devices have to be replaced often and old ones disposed of. But as you can see, they still have significant kick."

Malikovsky rode the elevator back to the lobby where Cherie waited with Guy. The three of them descended back to the basement. While Cherie led Guy from the elevator, Kroeker waited by the open metal lockers with the Geiger counter. Guy had barely gotten off the elevator when the rapid clicking stopped.

The administrator chuckled.

"You shut the detector off," he said merrily. He walked to a recessed panel in the wall and removed a hospital model scintillation reader and switched it on. He walked toward the lockers and his frown deepened. He passed the device over them, muttering to himself. He lowered it directly into one locker after the other before facing Malikovsky with a confused expression.

"It's a trick," he said at last. "What are you up to here?"

Malikovsky ignored the question. "How much does the disposal of waste like this cost?"

"You don't want to know, believe me."

Malikovsky's face darkened. "Yes, I do."

The administrator rocked back on his heels as if he'd been shoved.

"I can look up the exact numbers," he said. "Two hundred thousand a year, probably."

"Keep this load for a month," Malikovsky said. "Kroeker will check it weekly. And tell no one about this."

The administrator had a spark of terror in his eyes as he nodded. Cherie shivered so hard her knees banged together.

Now Kroeker was in the hotel suite struggling to explain his guess to Sergei, and Cherie felt the shiver anew. Despite many years working with Sergei, Kroeker still wrung his hands when Sergei glowered at him.

"How can I give you more than a guess? I'm an attorney, not a rocket scientist."

"And how does he do it?" Malikovsky demanded.

"I told you, I'm not a..."

"Not a rocket scientist," snorted Malikovsky. "That's obvious."

Then a smile played on his lips. He crossed the room and clasped Kroeker's shoulders.

"Let us celebrate for now," he said happily. "I forgive you for be-ing an idiot, the same way I forgive Cherie for being a bimbo. And myself for being greedy."

With this Malikovsky broke into a belly laugh, and the others tried to laugh with him.

*

Late that night Cherie answered a tentative knock at the door of the suite. Kroeker trudged into the living room area and went to the minibar. He poured two of the tiny bottles of vodka into a glass and spritzed club soda into it.

"Sergei's off to the airport," the attorney said, and poured most of the drink down his throat. "The mice could play, if they weren't so beat." He refilled the drink he hadn't finished yet and made one for Cherie. He clinked his glass to hers. "Here's to the mice of the world."

Cherie resumed painting her toenails. She was applying a new coat of deep pink.

"I'm not a mouse," she said.

Kroeker shrugged. "I am."

"Don't sell yourself short."

"I don't need to. Sergei takes care of that. The funny thing is that I was about to quit before this new business started. I'd had enough of Sergei, his temper..." Kroeker waved a long arm around ineffec-tually. "I've saved enough money."

"I haven't."

"I'm not the spendthrift you are."

"You're cheap, Bob."

He didn't argue it. "Do you know how I met Sergei?" he asked.

"You met him at your wife's funeral. She was Russian."

Kroeker walked to the minibar and fixed another drink.

"Hard to imagine me as a romantic, isn't it?" He tasted the new drink and added a spritz of water. "But I loved Irene. She wasn't a mail order bride, either. I happened to be in Moscow after the USSR collapsed, giving them advice on good old capitalism."

He dropped into the plush chair opposite Cherie's.

"I changed my mind about quitting because Guy came along."

Cherie paused in her work and looked over at him.

"Irene died of leukemia. She grew up near Chernobyl. Her bones were riddled with cancer. It's a miracle she lived as long as she did."

Cherie put the brush back in the bottle although three of her toenails were still their natural color. She steepled her hands over her perfect nose and gazed at him.

"Do you understand?" he asked. "It's because of Irene that I decided not to quit. After she died I didn't care about anything at all. Without her nothing else had value. But this boy, this Guy..." He looked into his drink and then at Cherie again. "Guy may be able to prevent what happened to Irene from happening to some other woman that some other man loves as much as I loved Irene."

Cherie nodded slowly.

"So I stay," Kroeker said, "even though I don't want to."

"I know," Cherie said softly.

"If it weren't for you I would have left a long time ago."

"I know," she said even more softly.

Kroeker met her eyes.

"The kid's getting to both of us, isn't he?" he said.

Cherie tilted her head and stared at the dimmed overhead light. She took a long breath.

"We shouldn't be talking about this," she whispered.

When he had left, Cherie went to the closed bedroom door at the far end of the living room. She listened for a moment and went in. She watched Guy sleeping and imagined what Sergei would say if he could read her mind.

*

Malikovsky returned the following afternoon, barking orders. By nightfall they were flying northward. In Portland they boarded a chartered helicopter. Guy slept most of the way, his head nestled in Cherie's lap.

Malikovsky, in the forward passenger seat, twisted his tree-trunk torso to look back at them.

"Kroeker, tell us what you know about the Hanford nuclear site."

"As I recall," Kroeker said, "they had the first nuclear reactors there. That was during the Cold War."

"Nine," said Malikovsky. "Nine reactors."

"The reactors made plutonium for warheads. The place is an environmental catastrophe. The Department of Energy has been trying to clean it up. That's about it." He hesitated. "As I said before..."

"You're not a rocket scientist," Cherie quipped, and elbowed him.

Malikovsky wagged a finger. "They have a hundred seventy-seven tanks of liquid radioactive waste. Fifty-three million gallons of toxic crap that will stay hot for half a million years, and it's leaking from the storage tanks. They're building a plant to vitrify it. Turn it into glass, so it will stop leaking. We are going to show them a better way."

Kroeker and Cherie went still. When Cherie spoke her voice was strained.

"You expect Guy to decontaminate all that tonight?"

"One tank tonight, that's all. It's mostly underground, but he can penetrate to the bottom. It's only fifty feet." A devious smile crossed his lips. "The first tank is done for free. After that one we name our own price."

Cherie was incredulous. "You're going to walk Guy across a cesspool of radioactive waste?"

"No." Malikovsky shook his head decisively. "You are."

"Sergei, we ought to consider..." Kroeker began.

"Listen to me, you putzers," Malikovsky hissed. "Every single atom of nuclear waste since the Manhattan Project is still in storage out there. Nobody—not the scientists who made it, not the government that paid for it, not the taxpayers who own it now—has any idea how to get rid of it. It's the worst poison in history. It's deadly for hundreds of thousands of years and it can't be destroyed."

He smacked a heavy palm on the top of his seat.

"You can use it for baby buggies after that kid works his magic! He's a golden goose! He's *our* golden goose! You better both grow bigger balls!"

He faced front again and the helicopter droned on.

*

Armed guards escorted them from the helipad to a makeshift office in a squat steel building that dated from the nineteen-fifties. Hanford looked like a small city camouflaged as a military installation. The landscape was high desert ringed by low ugly mountains. Cherie stepped onto the tarmac with a shudder, certain that the prickling she felt was radiation seeping into her skin. Guy leaned sleepily against her with one skinny arm wrapped around her waist.

Inside the office another man, this one in a civilian suit, joined them. The two guards brought up the rear as they trooped down a deserted street with lamps overhead glowing yellowish-green. Turning a corner, they came to an extended array of underground storage tanks. Protruding three feet above the ground, they resembled flattened toadstools stretching into the dark distance. The suited civilian pointed at the nearest one and departed into a warren of steel buildings. The two guards remained.

Cherie tried to back away but Malikovsky locked her shoulder in a steel grip.

"This isn't safe," she said. "I won't do it."

Malikovsky swore at her and Kroeker stepped forward.

"I'll go with the kid," he said.

Guy evaded him and wormed closer to Cherie. She stroked his head and gazed at the overcast sky. She drew a frightened breath.

"Come on, Guy," she said. "The sooner we do it, the sooner we leave this hellhole."

She walked to the steel plate top of the underground tank and stepped up onto it. She pulled Guy up beside her.

"Walk the perimeter of it first," Malikovsky said. "Then smaller circles until you stand in the middle. Get on with it."

Cherie suddenly turned back and tried to climb down, but Malikovsky moved forward faster. Her feet were still on the platform while her body leaned at an angle against his powerful arms.

"A hundred dollars a step!" he snarled. "Count!"

Pushing her to a vertical stance, he cracked her so sharply on the buttocks that her initial step was a hop. After that she hurried with Guy stumbling alongside.

With step number two hundred and thirteen they reached the screw-down hatch at the center, and Cherie half-dragged Guy to the edge and jumped with him to the ground.

"Six minutes," noted Kroeker. "Twenty-one thousand three hundred dollars."

"Don't expect me to do that again," Cherie told Malikovsky as they headed back.

Malikovsky planted his bulk in her path so fast that she and Guy could not avoid running into him. Malikovsky grabbed Cherie by the chin and squeezed so tightly that her lips mashed into a pucker. His voice lowered to a snarl.

"If you tell me again what you will or won't do, it'll be the end of your gravy train. I'll trade you to the Arabs for barrels of oil. They'll pass you on to the Congolese, and they'll pass you on to the Somalians, and when you're too diseased even for them they'll toss you to the sharks. Am I making myself clear?"

Cherie nodded as much as she was able. Malikovsky let go and patted her flushed cheek.

"I keep the twenty-one thousand as payment for your stupid remark."

"Yes, Sergei."

"And you work for free until this enterprise is finished."

"I will, Sergei."

"Now we go home."

Malikovsky swung about and struck a fast pace to where the helicopter waited.

*

A little after midnight Cherie glided naked from bed while Malikovsky snored. She slipped into her silk kimona and quietly closed the door behind her. From the wet bar in the living room she retrieved her favorite vodka and sat down at the glass-topped table on the terrace. After two swallows from the bottle she replaced the cap and set it down. Cherie was a perceptive woman and knew it, but she wasn't a deep thinker and realized that, too. When her mind was troubled, she turned her attention to buying an expensive present for herself. By the time she finished the shopping for it her mind was at peace again. It worked like magic and she was secretly proud of the method. In her private opinion, only masochists tried to work out their troubles by thinking about them.

That opinion she kept to herself, because Cherie didn't believe in sharing opinions. Everyone was entitled to their own opinion and everyone had their own. What could possibly be gained by telling them to someone else? What now troubled her mind was that she had an opinion that she wouldn't be able to shop into silence. It was like a bomb in her trying to explode.

Cherie opened the bottle again but this time took only a sip. She recapped it and wondered if she could wake Kroeker, because he would listen. She decided against it. Although she wanted to voice her opinion she also wanted its secrecy preserved.

When she realized what she was going to do she fortified herself with two more swallows of the vodka and carried the bottle with her. She listened for Sergei's snoring before stealing into Guy's bedroom at the far end of the suite. With faint illumination from California Street below, shadows moved silently on the white walls. Cherie sat on the edge of the bed and tentatively touched his pale cheek. He stirred but didn't wake until she whispered his name. With that he quickly sat up, blinking. When she recognized Cherie he gave a little smile and lay back.

"You don't talk much, do you, Guy?" she asked.

His expression became very serious and he gave a quick shake of his head.

"Guy. Do you know what autism is?"

His eyes flitted to the side.

"The doctor who helps at St. Catherine's says you're autistic. Is that true, do you think?" She laid her palm on his chest and rubbed in a circular motion. "I don't mind if you are. In this case, it would be a good thing, because I'm going to tell you something and I don't want you to ever tell anyone else that I said it. Okay?"

Finally he met her eyes again. He tightened his lips together and gave a short nod.

"Sergei is a jackass," she said.

Guy nodded solemnly. Cherie felt herself starting to cry. She wiped the tears away without embarrassment.

"Sometimes I hate him," she said. "I hope he burns in hell. When he dies I'm going to go to his grave and pee on it and I hope he's burning in hell and can see me doing it."

Cherie took a long breath, feeling much better already. She sniffed and wiped her eyes once more and noticed that Guy was silently laughing.

"You think that's funny, huh?" When Guy nodded, she said, "I guess it would make a funny sight, me pulling up my dress and squatting on his grave and peeing." She felt a sudden pang of worry. "Please don't tell anyone what I said. I just wanted to say it."

She leaned down and kissed Guy on the forehead. She leaned down again and kissed him on the nose. When he shut his eyes and pushed his lips together, she leaned down a third time and gave his mouth a soft kiss that lingered a moment longer than she intended. Afterward he kept his eyes shut and an impish smile came and went and returned again. His hands pushed open the top of her kimona and cupped her breasts.

"You naughty boy," Cherie whispered. "I told you not to fall in love with me."

With a stricken look on his face he withdrew his hands.

"No, no," she assured him. "It's all right. I was being… ironic." Cherie wasn't sure that word was the correct one. "I like that you're in love with me. It makes me feel… safe." This time she was quite sure she had the correct word.

She shifted her position sideways to face him more directly, with her right leg on the bed, her knee cocked against his hip. His pale blue eyes met hers. Then his gaze traveled down her body and fixed on where the lower part of her kimona had fallen open.

Cherie reached for the vodka bottle on the nightstand and got the cap off and took a swallow that burned her throat because it was swollen from crying. His hand had moved into her lap and now glided through the opening of the kimona. She felt very loose, as if someone had untied all the knots that held her together, but she didn't mind. She felt more like herself than she had ever felt before.

"Do you want me to come into bed with you?" she asked.

Guy averted his eyes before giving a short nod. For a moment Cherie wondered if her good feeling meant that she was losing her mind.

"Well, then, let's not disappoint you," she said. Undoing the belt of her kimona, she dropped it to the floor. She slid under the covers and kissed him again.

*

Malikovsky launched the second phase of his scheme. He formed a corporation and applied for the federal licenses necessary to do nuclear remediation. With hefty campaign donations here and there, the applications sailed through. Licenses in hand, Malikovsky offered Guy's services to the private sector. Nuclear waste of any kind would be neutralized.

There were plenty of takers. General Electric and Dow had obligations to clean up Superfund sites where they had done nuclear work and they jumped at the opportunity to clear the liabilities from their books. The nuclear-powered electrical utilities also wasted no time signing contracts, and they were followed by counties and states with contamination issues.

There was radioactive waste accumulated in more places than even Malikovsky had dreamed. The federal government had a hundred sites so contaminated that they were permanently closed to public access. They contained thousands of tons of spent nuclear fuel, millions of gallons of radioactive liquids, and billions of cubic yards of toxic debris and dirt. There were some efforts being made to "clean up" the worst locations, but that was merely a euphemism for "moving the contamination somewhere else."

Where to move it was the question. Clean-up entailed separating out the radioactive isotopes from whatever material they contaminated. The essence could then be sealed in containers and stored in salt mine caves or dry oil wells, where hopefully it would be undisturbed for several hundred thousand years. This was hardly an ideal solution.

Malikovsky set his price high, and charged by the cubic yard. He didn't distinguish between high-level and low-level waste for the simple reason that it didn't matter to Guy. The boy could extinguish radiation of a hundred tons of crated plutonium fuel rods in a half-minute by walking around it, while walking over a hundred acres to decontaminate soil and groundwater could take all afternoon.

From the first batch of spent fuel rods that Guy decontaminated, Malikovsky had a plutonium ring made. He brandished it on his right hand as a visual aid in contract negotiations. It worked better than words.

*

The days of Guy watching nature programs on the Discovery channel came to an abrupt end. In spite of official silence from the Nuclear Regulatory Commission, news of the miracle at Hanford raced through the industry—a cure had been found for the scourge of radiation. With Guy's services suddenly in demand, the applicants engaged in bidding wars.

Malikovsky leased a Lear jet for travel. He gave Kroeker responsibility for the itinerary and Cherie the responsibility for Guy. For her that meant waking Guy when it was barely light and keeping him cooperative until late in the evening, while fitting in meals and getting him enough sleep.

"What about child labor laws?" she ventured to ask.

Sergei scoffed. "Labor? The boy's not working. He's touring the country. Sightseeing isn't against the law."

"What about the law saying he has to attend school?"

"He's being home-schooled. Right now he's learning geography."

The geography lessons came fast and furious. In two weeks they visited six states. Kroeker was also compiling a list of overseas applicants. Every nuclear power facility in the world had waste ponds and spent reactor rods—four-hundred thirty-six operative reactors in all.

At the end of June, Japan offered a billion dollars for Malikovsky and his team to come visit as honored guests for a week and tour their nuclear plants. France followed it with an offer of two billion. Russia offered five billion for a two week visit.

By mid-summer Guy had been nicknamed. The nuclear industry had anointed him with the title of "The Plutonium Kid."

*

For every enthusiastic fan of the Plutonium Kid there was also a detractor. The skeptics said that it was scientifically impossible to neutralize radiation—physics simply didn't allow it. Here they had a point. As the assistant researcher from Stanford had tried to explain, radiation is really of two types. The first type is excited atoms releasing photons of light. Light is radiation, but it isn't a concern as long as the photons don't have high energy. When they do, they're destructive to the human body. Those high-energy photons are called gamma rays or x-rays.

The second type of radiation occurs when parts of an atomic nucleus break free and fly away. Such nuclear decay occurs in very heavy atoms like uranium, which have lots of nuclear particles and have trouble holding onto them all. Elements of this kind are called unstable, but the degree of instability varies. In some, the atoms may decay in milliseconds, while in others atoms decay over billions of years. Fast or slow, however, all nuclear decay damages living tissue. Escaping particles carry so much kinetic energy that when they crash into cells it's like cannonballs hitting wet tissue paper. No matter whether the cannonballs are high-energy photons of radiated light or particles from an atomic nucleus, radiation kills.

Guy's detractors denied that he could neutralize either type. They insisted that nuclear decay was a physical fact of reality and to stop it was like stopping gravity. Furthermore, to stop x-rays or gamma rays was like stopping the sun from shining.

Both their contentions were correct. Nevertheless, they couldn't win the debate, because Guy was indeed doing what they said he couldn't. While one can argue that events shouldn't happen, one can't hope to win the argument when they do. When theory doesn't match up with reality, it is the theory that has to change, because reality won't. Physicists went to work on the problem.

The most plausible hypothesis offered was that somehow Guy was pulling zero-point energy out of the fabric of space-time and stabilizing the radiating atoms with it. It sounded crazy even to those who proposed it, but so did most of modern physics, so that favored its credibility. The core idea was that nuclear decay was caused by random fluctuations in space-time. The nucleus of a heavy atom was like a big house-of-cards. It was so complex that it was inherently unstable. The smallest disturbance would make its awkward structure shift and a particle would escape the nuclear bonds holding it in place. Where would the nudge come from? From fluctuations in the zero-point energy. That is to say, from infinitesimal bubbles in space-time.

Thus, Guy was somehow drawing energy from space-time emptiness—and energy was there, even detractors acknowledged that—to stabilize the heavy atoms. He used the zero-point energy as glue to hold the house-of-cards together. The house couldn't easily collapse anymore and the nuclei wouldn't decay.

The hypothesis also explained how he blocked x-rays. Stability in the radiating nuclei meant they could hold onto high-energy photons while letting regular light escape. The more energy a photon had, the less likely it would escape.

*

None of this made sense to Cherie and she didn't have time to ponder it. Handling Guy was hard enough. When under stress he automatically reached for her breasts, and if she was wearing a skirt his hand disappeared under it. He didn't comprehend the neater points of social etiquette, which people didn't always understand. Furthermore, long days wore him out, yet he was unable to sleep unless Cherie slept alongside. This made her unavailable for Sergei. He grumbled about it, but not excessively. Cherie didn't need to remind him that without her company Guy was like an unplugged money machine.

Through July the money machine handed out cash as fast as Malikovsky could count it.

*

Late that month the sheriff served a subpoena. The St. Catherine's Orphanage for Children had filed a complaint in District Court. The Catholic diocese running the orphanage asked that the adoption of Guy L. Strange be rejected, arguing it was based on fraudulent statements by the adoptive parents. The complaint asserted that Sergei and Cherie had no interest in parenting the boy, only in exploiting his hidden talent. It further asserted that exposure to radiation risked his long-term health.

Malikovsky stomped across the suite with the legal papers wadded in one meaty fist.

"The Pope put them up to it!" he bellowed. "That greedy bastard wants to get his hands on the cash flow, that's all! Did he care when his priests molested those altar boys? No! Did the Church care about the Jews in Poland? No! Did the Church ever given a damn about anything but money and power? No! And it doesn't care about this boy, this poor boy who would have no family or home if it weren't for me." He stabbed his index finger in the air, "It only cares about the profits the orphan earns. The Pope can go to hell! Who does he think he's fooling with?"

Malikovsky then levelled his fury at Kroeker.

"What are you going to do about this?" he demanded, shoving the papers in his face.

Kroeker carefully flattened them out on the coffee table.

"Sergei," he said, "I will fight it."

"Of course you'll fight it, you idiot! But can you win? Can we keep the boy or not?"

"We're entitled to a six month trial period. If we can convince the court there's no imminent threat to Guy's well-being, we can at least keep him until that's over."

"And what happens then?" Sergei blustered.

"The court will evaluate Guy, also the stability of your marriage to Cherie, also the claim that the adoption was a sham. I hate to say this, Sergei, but the court will probably want to know just how much the boy has earned during the six months and how you invested it for him. It will take a dim view of the fact that the earnings are all in our pockets rather than in a trust for Guy. But," he added quickly, "I can draw up a trust assigning half the net income to Guy..."

"Ten percent!"

"That's not sufficient. It has to be at least half. But I'll ask that you be made executor of the trust until Guy can function independently. With his autism, that would be never."

Malikovsky glowered and stomped a little more, but with less force.

"Here's what you have to remember, Sergei. The Church will hire private investigators to dig into your business dealings. And Cherie's past, which has been—colorful, to put it mildly. It will be hard to persuade the court you have Guy's best intentions at heart. We can appeal if the judge rules against us, of course. But in the end?" He paused. "In the end, they will take Guy away."

"So we have him for four more months," Malikovsky said bitterly.

Kroeker shifted uncomfortably. "My guess is the Church already has investigators searching for whatever dirt they can find. I worry about what they'll find. The court may send Guy back to the orphanage after the hearing, which is only two weeks away."

"They won't," Malikovsky vowed. "Watch and see. I'm not a naïve altar boy."

*

An hour later Malikovsky and Cherie applied for a passport for Guy.

That was all it took for the Federal Government to act. Turf battles between federal agencies had prevented prior action. But with the likelihood of the Plutonium Kid traveling to countries where he might be taken hostage, government agencies and regulators found common cause.

On the third of August, Malikovsky met with a score of officials in a hotel conference room. Representatives from the Departments of Energy, Defense, and Homeland Security attended the meeting. The Nuclear Regulatory Commission and Environmental Protection Agency both had seats at the tables, as well as the CIA, FBI, and NSA.

It promised to be a long and noisy meeting.

The head of Homeland Security gave the opening statement. In it he announced that under no circumstances would Guy get a passport.

Malikovsky lumbered to his feet before the man could go any further. Raising his right hand, Malikovsky rotated it so that everyone got a good look at the massive ring on his third finger.

"This ring," he rumbled, "is six ounces of pure plutonium. It is mine. But it is different than the ten thousand tons of plutonium belonging to you people. Do you know why? Because it is harmless. *Your* plutonium is deadly. There's enough of your plutonium to kill life on the planet many times over. *My* plutonium is harmless. That is why you will listen to what *I* say instead of me listening to you. We can all get what we want out of this meeting. But if you refuse to listen, you will walk out of here with nothing."

The officials had come into the conference room with contempt for a Russian buffoon. They left believing that Malikovsky was a courageous American patriot.

The bargain he made was this: Guy wouldn't leave United States soil until he had treated all the contaminated Superfund sites and all radioactive waste at the one-hundred and eight nuclear plants. He would finish with the Herculean task within four months. His passport would then be issued and he would be free to travel for nuclear remediation in friendly nations. Meanwhile the federal government would ensure that the trial adoption period lasted the full six months before the District Court issued a decision.

Malikovsky didn't bother mentioning that as soon as the passport was issued, he and Cherie and Guy would leave the country. They would be earning billion dollar fees in other countries, far beyond the reach of any US court. When they did return, it would be because all the nuclear remediation on the globe was finished. If the Church still demanded Guy after that, they could have him. The money machine would be out of cash. The Pope could wail and gnash his teeth until hell froze.

Malikovsky explained it that way to Kroeker after coming back up to the hotel suite.

"Sergei," the attorney said, "that's over two hundred sites. How can Guy manage all that in four months? He'll have to cover hundreds of acres on some of them."

Malikovsky waved his plutonium-ringed hand. "We put him into a jeep and drive across the site as fast as terrain allows. We cover two sites a day. Draw up a map that minimizes distance between sites. We finish in less than four months."

"Isn't that asking a lot of a sixteen-year old?"

"At sixteen I could wrestle elephants," Malikovsky answered. "When Cherie gets back with the boy, tell her to pack. We leave tonight."

*

Cherie had taken Guy to her favorite spot in San Francisco. To her, Golden Gate Park was a sanctuary where she could breathe fresh air instead of the stench of corruption that permeated the circles she usually traveled in. The long rectangular park, designed to rival Central Park in New York City, extended westward all the way to the Pacific Ocean, almost bisecting the city.

From the Mark Hopkins they rode a cable car down Powell to Market and boarded a city bus that dropped them at the Panhandle, a strip of greenery poking out of the eastern end of the park. Fortified with ice cream cones, they strolled down a meandering asphalt path, through a tunnel, and then under towering trees toward the Steinhart Museum.

Guy's pale triangular face showed no emotion, but he hurried from the window of one display case to the next, staring mutely at the tarantulas and frogs and lizards and snakes while he rubbed his mouth with his slender fingers.

After they had traveled from entrance to exit, he grabbed Cherie's hand and dragged her back to the entrance again. This time through he occasionally glanced at Cherie as if curious whether the exotic creatures were as fascinating to her as they were to him. She knew that autists tended to be oblivious to the inner lives of other people. But wasn't it remotely possible that Guy really did recognize her as a human being in her own right? The consideration brought a genuine smile to her face. Was an autistic boy the only person in the world who noticed she had a human soul under the superficial appearance that bedazzled men? Her heart lightened and she shivered with excitement. She ached with the thought of how many hours remained in the day.

After the Aquarium they stood in line for the laser show at the Planetarium. The colors that darted in spirals and arcs and waves transfixed Guy. In the darkness they held hands like lovers while the fantastic lights danced on the ceiling and Beethoven's Fifth boomed at them from all directions.

Outside again the sun was stunningly bright, so they took turns wearing Cherie's wraparound sunglasses. No one in the crowds of park visitors had approached Guy, but any number of times had given him long stares, and after a few minutes Cherie let him keep the sunglasses. They hid the strange distance in his eyes, so that he looked a normal schoolboy in the company of his big sister and not the star child who was revolutionizing nuclear physics.

"Now," she said in a stage whisper, "we're going to see a herd of real buffalo!"

To speed him to a brisk pace she gave him a teasing pinch on the buttocks.

The couple that approached them looked like tourists from the Midwest.

"It's our little Guy!" the woman exclaimed. She poked an elbow in the man's paunchy side. "I told you it was him! It is him!"

The woman herself was thin as a stalk of wheat, but a laxity in her skin suggested that she had once been much heavier. She was plain-faced, but the vivacity there gave her appearance such a boost that Cherie could imagine her in a romantic movie. The man, despite a balding pate and thickness at the belt line, looked like an aging Valentino. He had bent down to study Guy with an analytic frown.

"We were the ones who found him," the woman said with maternal pride. "Just a baby lying all alone on the mountain without even a blanket. Henri saw him first. Didn't you, Henri? Oh, I'm Marie Le Strange. That's Henri, he's a nuclear physicist, isn't that right, Henri? He teaches at Stanford and knows all about Guy's miracles. We're tickled to see our boy face-to-face again! I held him in my arms not so long ago and now look at him!"

Sensing that she was about to embrace the boy, Cherie maneuvered between them.

"What brings you to the park?" she inquired.

"Well, we didn't expect this! But, Henri! Did we expect to find him that first time? No, we did not. I almost believed he'd fallen from a golden chariot in the sky!"

"This is where we came on our first date," Henri said, tapping a foot on the grassy hillock on which they stood. "We were impoverished university students and we came over from Berkeley for a picnic. Every August we celebrate the anniversary."

"We had a bottle of wine and drank it all and got turned around and ended up here on Hippie Hill, didn't we, Henri?"

Cherie's suspicions waned. She made them retell the tale of finding Guy.

"So you are..." Marie looked flummoxed, unable to complete the sentence because she hadn't completed it in her mind first. "You are... what? Guy's... Not his mother?"

Henri said, "Unless she's kidnapped him, Marie, I think that's exactly who she is."

"Ah." Marie smiled uncertainly. "You seem so happy together. I thought you might be his girlfriend. I can't help it. I'm an incurable romantic on the subject of love. Henri and I, we fell in love when we weren't even looking, didn't we, Henri?"

All through this chatting Guy kept cocking his head one way and then the other way. After a while he wandered further up the hill and stood gazing in the direction from which he and Cherie had come.

"Hush, Marie," Henri said. "Go over and talk to Guy. He might not talk back, but I'll bet he listens fine." When Marie was out of earshot, Henri changed from his good-natured professorial attitude to that of a no-nonsense scientist. "Listen closely to me," he said in a low tone to Cherie, "because we've only got a minute before she comes back and I would rather not worry her about the boy who is in love with you." He paused there as if letting her know she had no secrets from him. "I haven't figured out how Guy accomplishes what he does, but I know that radiation can't be neutralized. Not by man, not by God, and I assure you not by an autistic youth. I don't think it's a parlor trick. That means whatever he's really doing is danger-ous. It is going to kill him if you don't stop it. Do you understand? It will kill him."

Cherie, confused by the quiet anger, drew back a step.

"He's fine," she said. "Doctors checked him. He doesn't absorb any radiation at all."

"He can't be fine, no matter what the doctors say," Henri said in a clipped voice. "Watch him closely for any signs of illness, any changes in behavior."

Henri started to say more but glanced over his shoulder first and shook his head. Turning, he opened his arms to Marie. As the two hugged, Cherie drew Guy protectively close.

"Okay!" she said cheerfully. "Isn't it time we ate ice cream again?"

*

Malikovsky's confidence in Guy was amazing, considering the low esteem he had for human beings in general, and through the summer Guy validated it. From dawn until evening day after day without rest, Guy performed his miracles. With Cherie at his side and Kroeker at the wheel, he sped down silent streets, over toxic fields, across contaminated streams. Behind him he left a pristine environ-ment with not a curie of radiation.

They had started in the Northwest, again at the vast Hanford site. There they spent two days and afterward the technicians and bureau-crats and anti-nuclear activists stared at their detectors in disbelieving wonder. At the open-pit Anaconda mine in Nevada the same hap-pened, and also at the Rocketdyne site in southern California. Kroeker's meticulous itinerary carried them from one small rural airport to another in their leased Lear jet, stitching an erratic but efficient pattern across the country.

In Oak Ridge, Tennessee, home of the Manhattan Project of the 1940's, their rapid progress abruptly stopped. Guy collapsed halfway through a bag of Cheetos.

Cherie raced him to the infirmary. The duty nurse diagnosed his condition as exhaustion, as she could discover no better explanation. There was no fever, no evidence of radiation sickness, no pain, nausea, or breathing problem, but Guy's eyes were glazed and he was too weak to walk.

Malikovsky paced in wordless apprehension. Afterward they retired to the Holiday Inn where they had rooms. Guy slept. Kroeker phoned for a pizza delivery. The three adults drank Cokes and ate their slices in gloomy silence.

"We're a day ahead of schedule," Malikovsky said. "We'll take the afternoon off. Start fresh tomorrow. Kroeker, you rent an SUV. We fold the back seat down. The boy doesn't have to be sitting or watching. He can rest while we drive, sleep if he wants."

"Sergei, that might not be wise," Kroeker objected. "We don't even know what's wrong with him."

"You heard the nurse, he's tired. When you're tired you rest. He can rest in a moving car."

Kroeker glanced at Cherie, who had stopped eating her slice of pizza.

"But if he gets sicker..." Kroeker said.

"We have a month to go," Malikovsky said, "with sixteen sites left. Guy can have a vacation when he's done. End of discussion."

*

Instead of improving, Guy's condition worsened. By October he was gaunt and listless. He slept at night with intermittent jerks of his muscles as if fighting an unseen enemy in his dreams. Cherie spoonfed him soup and baby food and chewable vitamins in an effort to keep his strength up and held his hand while he was driven back and forth across sites, but the day came that he no longer responded even to her considerable persuasions.

Cherie reached the voice mail of Henri le Strange through his extension at Stanford. Waiting in the motel restaurant for a return call, she pushed the remains of a green salad around her plate. The call came an hour later as she was returning to their room.

As she related the update on Guy's condition she began crying.

"I thought Guy was going into a coma," she told him, dabbing at her eyes with a corner of her silk scarf. "Sergei told me to kiss him on the lips. He told me I was like a princess and Guy was under a spell. You don't know Sergei. He actually makes you believe ridiculous things like that. So I did it. I gave Guy a kiss on the lips. He looked so helpless lying there."

"And did it work?" Henri asked.

Cherie fought a sob. "He kissed me back. Hardly at all, but now Sergei says we're doing the last two sites tomorrow. He says Guy can have a month vacation in France after that, but I don't know if Guy can do even one more day. What do you think?"

"You're legally his mother, aren't you?" Henri asked. "Why don't you get Guy in a taxi and take him to the hospital?"

Cherie gave a brittle laugh. "I don't think so. I've seen what happens when someone crosses Sergei. They end up dead or worse." She glanced toward the room where Kroeker was keeping a vigil on Guy. "After tomorrow we fly to San Francisco to collect Guy's passport. Then we fly to Europe for what Sergei is calling the World Tour. Could you come to San Francisco and take a look at Guy while we're there? You're a doctor, right?"

Henri explained he was a doctor but not a physician.

"Real doctors are useless," Cherie told him. "He's been to three and they can't find anything wrong with him." She waved to Kroeker as he emerged from the room and scanned the parking lot. "I'll call you when we get to San Fran," she said.

Walking to the room, Cherie had a lighter step. It was risky going behind Sergei's back and calling Henri, but it felt liberating. Hours earlier she had wanted to take Guy to the hospital and Kroeker had agreed. When they told Malikovsky he listened calmly, massaging

114

his boulder-like chin. After they were done he sighed and looked out the motel window.

"We've made much money in these months—more than we can spend in ten lifetimes. Ten percent is yours, Kroeker. And Cherie knows she has ten percent, no matter what I said when I was angry. You will both be billionaires. If we continue, it isn't for the money. Agreed?"

Kroeker cleared his throat and nodded. Cherie, who had expected no compensation because of the incident at Hanford, blinked with surprise.

Malikovsky faced them. He opened his hands. "We are rich. The boy can take a rest if that is truly necessary. But there is a problem. We cannot leave this country until we have finished the last two sites. And if we are not gone by the first of November we need to appear in District Court for the adoption hearing. We will be accused of exploiting the boy for our personal profit. The judge won't care that we have saved ninety-nine percent of the United States from the curse of radiation. He will revoke the adoption. The boy will go back to the orphanage."

Malikovsky shrugged heavily.

"So here is our choice. We can retire as billionaires and not be concerned that all the rest of the world suffers from radioactivity until the end of time. Is that what we want? Or we can have Guy work one more day so we can get his passport. Then we can leave and save the rest of the world. Which will it be? It is time for us to take a vote."

Cherie knew Kroeker's thoughts. He was thinking of his dead wife Irene and the millions of other well-loved women who might die of radioactive poisoning. If she voted against doing the last two sites, she would be standing alone, because Kroeker would side with Sergei. She could hardly think. It was impossible to clear her head of the dizzying knowledge that she was now one of the wealthiest women in the world. She was free for the first time in her life to say no to what she disliked and say yes to whatever pleased her. That Malikovsky was manipulating them both with his implacable logic barely registered in her thinking. She voted with Kroeker to have Guy work one more day.

Entering the motel room where the boy slept, she felt elated. Yes, she had let Sergei bribe her with a billion dollars to betray her better instincts. But now that she had asked for Henri's help, she had taken a small step to regain her self-respect. She was determined to take as many steps as necessary to earn it all back.

*

Henri came to the Mark Hopkins suite after Malikovsky bustled off to collect Guy's passport at the San Francisco Federal Building. He passed a glance at their packed suitcases standing by the door and then let Cherie lead him to Guy's room. The boy was tossing spasmodically on his bed, flinging his arms and kicking his legs. His eyes rolled back and weird groans escaped his throat. Henri shoved his scarf in his suitcoat pocket.

"How long has he been like this?"

"It started a half hour ago."

Henry felt the boy's brow. He measured his pulse, checked his tongue, and then palpated his abdomen.

"We need to get him to a hospital."

Cherie caught a sob in her throat. "Should I call an ambulance?"

"No. We'll take him in my car to UC Medical."

Henri got an arm around the boy's back and the other behind his knees and lifted him bodily. Kroeker ran ahead for the elevator while Cherie held the hall door, and they were shortly in the lobby with tourists staring as they hurried past.

Henri carried Guy down the curved steps with Cherie supporting the boy's head in her hands. They were headed for the Lexus parked at the curb when Malikovsky stepped out of a Yellow Cab. The Russian absorbed the scene in a split second and swore with vehemence.

"Who is this man and where is he going with my son?" he demanded, striding on an interception course.

Kroeker stepped in his path.

"He's taking him to the hospital, Sergei. He's taking him…"

They were the last words Kroeker ever spoke. Malikovsky was three hundred pounds moving at full speed, and when he straight-armed Kroeker the lawyer reeled into the street. He stumbled past the Lexus, tried to regain his balance, tripped over his lanky legs, and fell headlong into the passing cable car. His body bounced off with a terrible thwack, limbs flying in every direction, and tumbled head over heels for a dozen yards.

Cherie clutched her hands in her hair and screamed. Malikovsky shoved her away as well and he and Henri struggled over possession of Guy.

"Stand aside, you damned fool," Henri shouted.

Cherie hurled herself onto Malikovsky's back and dug her fingers into his jowls, groping for his eyes, and with her sudden weight Malikovsky staggered backward. He recovered and gave a powerful shake like a grizzly bear shedding water. Cherie flew to one side, hitting the sidewalk head and shoulders first. Sergie kicked her.

"You stupid cow!" he shouted, and stomped on her furiously. "You're fired! Fired!"

Henri was struggling to get Guy into the backseat of the Lexus. Tourists and hotel staff had gathered in a half-circle around the scene, the cable car had come to a stop just beyond Kroeker's broken body, and sirens wailed from downtown.

As Henri straightened up Malikovsky closed the gap between them. The Russian grabbed the physicist with one hand and lifted him off the sidewalk. He drew back his plutonium-ringed fist to hammer Henri's face.

The blow never came. Malikovsky suddenly screamed. It began as a guttural bellow but rose in register until it was a full-throated shriek of agony that crested somewhere over Nob Hill. He dropped Henri and spun about in a circle, gripping his right hand with his left and waggling them both. He fell to his knees and bent forward, then raised up his enormous head and howled like a mortally wounded animal.

"My ring!" he screamed. "My ring is on fire! Mother of God, someone get it off!"

It was plain to see why he couldn't get the ring off himself. The plutonium had turned red-hot, so that every time he tried to pull it loose the heat scorched the fingers he touched it with.

And now as he danced about, waving his right hand madly over his head in the vain hope of cooling the ring, puffs of black smoke spread in the air. The reddened ring turned to a brilliant white, with glittering sparks flying from it, and an instant later Malikovsky's entire hand burst into flames. Unearthly strangled screams rose from his throat as he pounded the burning hand against the concrete sidewalk.

It was this awful image that met Cherie's eyes when she opened her eyes, and she scrabbled away as fast as she could. She didn't get to her feet until she backed into Henri, who had fallen against the Lexus and now stared in mute horror at the bear-like body writhing on the sidewalk. Smoke rose in black tendrils from all over Malikovsky's limbs and torso, and flames danced in his hair. A hotel bellhop arrived with a fire extinguisher and bathed the fiery figure in bubbling white foam as patrol cars screeched to the curb. Police immediately set up a cordon and pushed the gawkers back. Emergency workers clustered about Malikovsky, but in spite of the retardant foam the corpse still blazed like a bonfire.

"Why is his ring doing that?" Cherie asked, shuddering. "How can it burn him up like that?"

As she spoke a hand grasped at her and she jumped in alarm.

"Guy!"

The boy leaned out of the back seat of the Lexus, pale face thrust forward. His one hand took Cherie's and with the other he braced himself on the doorframe. Trembling and ghostly pale, he looked as if he had risen from his deathbed by an act of will. But it was the expression on Guy's face that stunned Henri. He showed neither shock nor horror at the sight of Sergei Malikovsky's smoldering body. Rather, he had the triumphant look of a white knight who has slain the dragon attacking his fair maiden.

*

Winter rain drizzled steadily on the December afternoon when Henri again rode the elevator of the Mark Hopkins. This time he took it to the top floor. As he stepped into the hall, he was met and frisked by guards. With polite efficiency they verified his identification before allowing him entry to the penthouse suite. Cherie welcomed him in with a grateful hug and a kiss to his cheek. Guy sprawled on the leather sofa watching a National Geographic show about chimpanzees, and Cherie ruffled his hair as she went by while leading Henri to the kitchen. There they shared a pot of tea, fresh fruit, and a basket of chocolate biscotti.

"Thank you for coming, Henri," she said. "I hope they didn't force you to come. I made it very clear that your visit should be voluntary."

"They treated me like an ambassador," he told her.

"I must remember to thank them."

Henri was surprised at Cherie's grasp of the situation. It had taken only a week or so for her to intuit what had happened and what it meant. The questions she asked him concerned the why of the events, and his explanations confirmed what she already suspected.

Henri, of course, had known the truth as soon as the plutonium ring blazed with white flames. Guy hadn't been neutralizing radiation, not in Malikovsky's ring and not in sites he had visited. He had only postponed the nuclear decays that threw off radiation.

The physics of it was simple. Nuclear decay was probabilistic. The chance of any particular atom decaying and radiating was mathematically determined, but no one could say exactly when it would happen. It was like rolling a die—any given number would come up a sixth of the time, but it was impossible to say how many rolls it might take to get, say, a one. It might come up on the first roll or it might come up on the thirtieth. Guy hadn't changed the probability of nuclear decay. He had only postponed that outcome.

How he managed to do it was unknown. Physicists had assumed that no one could affect the actions of subatomic particles. It was thought impossible. Now they talked about unconscious quantum entanglement. But was it unconscious? Certainly when Malikovsky attacked Cherie, Guy proved he could reverse the effect.

When he did, normal probabilities were restored. The rate of nuclear decay skyrocketed as all the delayed outcomes of the previous six months resumed. Billions of atoms in the ring decayed and spewed radiation. The ring got as hot as the sun's surface.

119

"Sergei had this weird idea about time," Cherie said. "He criticized other people for wanting to slow it down or stop it. But that's just what he was trying to do. Nuclear decay is like a clock, isn't it? An atomic clock? Even if you stop it, it's going to catch up as soon as it gets a chance."

For a minute they sat at the table in silence. Henri forked a slice of nectarine on his biscotti. He studied it from various angles before taking a careful bite. Cherie held her teacup in front of her, sipping it as she watched Henri.

"They're afraid of Guy, aren't they?" she asked.

"You saw what Guy did to Sergei's ring," Henri said. "He could do the same trick with any of the nuclear waste he treated. He could start meltdowns without lifting a finger."

"They won't try to kill him, will they?"

Henri used the hand holding his biscotti to wave the notion off. "Not a chance. If Guy died, his magic effect on decay probability would end. All those two hundred seventeen sites that he visited, they'd become catastrophes as bad as Chernobyl. Tanks filled with liquid waste would melt. Sludge pools would boil. Plutonium rods would explode like hydrogen bombs. It would be apocalyptic. Fallout would blanket the entire North American continent. Hundreds of millions would die in the first week alone. It's unthinkable."

Henri drained the last of his tea and set the cup down.

"So they can't let anything happen to Guy. He will be catered to and cared for as no man has ever been in the history of the planet. And as long as Guy wants you with him, you will be too."

Cherie gave Henri a speculative look.

"Henri, let me now ask this, which is why I invited you here. Are scientists working on a way to prevent all that from happening? Guy isn't going to live forever."

Henri's smile was bitter. "It isn't the scientists that matter, Cherie. It's the politicians, and all they care about is the next re-election. They've done nothing and they won't. They pretend the problem doesn't exist and they don't want anyone else to know about it."

She nodded thoughtfully.

"Do you think they need a little reminder?" she asked.

Henri glanced around the kitchen circumspectly before looking at her again. His nod was slight but unmistakable.

"Guy will know what to do," Cherie said. "He's quite clever."

Henri stood. Cherie walked him to the living room, where he paused to say hello to Guy, and then to the hall door. She fussed with his scarf and bestowed another kiss on his cheek.

"They're moving us next week, Henri, to a safer place. We won't be able to have visitors, but they promise we'll be treated like royalty."

"Won't you get lonely?" Henri asked. "Even if you love him, the king is still just a boy."

"But I'm so tired of men." Her full lips parted in a mischievous smile. "And Guy is always so eager to please me."

When Henri still seemed unconvinced, Cherie tilted her head and pushed back the cascade of honey-blonde hair that descended across the side of her face.

"Henri," she said, squeezing his hands, "when a whore is treated like a queen, she doesn't miss the other beds she slept in. Trust me, we're very happy together."

*

During the early morning of New Year's Day, one of the underground tanks at Hanover overheated in a supercritical reaction. It was the same tank that Guy had neutralized in the first test of his abilities. Remarkably, no one was injured. Equally remarkable was the fact that the reaction spontaneously subsided after a few hours. On January second, a second tank went supercritical. On January third, a third one did the same. Billions of curies of radiation were vented into the atmosphere with the unexplained accidents. Even the corrupt Nuclear Regulatory Commission couldn't contain the news. The President spoke darkly of domestic nuclear terrorism. No one publicly mentioned the name of the Plutonium Kid, who was officially dead.

*

That is how the unofficial story ends. I have set it down as it was told to me. If it is true, nuclear apocalypse is only a heartbeat away. That's not an easy idea to accept. Should we instead believe the official story, knowing it comes from a government that lies to us without the least hesitation?

When deciding between the unthinkable and the untrustworthy, it is advisable to seek supporting evidence for one or the other. In that regard, recent news stories are helpful. With a vote that is otherwise inexplicable, Congress last month quadrupled the budget of the Department of Energy. In the same legislation, a conference of nuclear scientists was scheduled for the spring. Discussions will include the feasibility of launching nuclear waste into space, preferably by constructing a carbon nanotube space elevator for that purpose.

What hasn't been in the news is also of interest. Nobody is making baby buggies out of the nuclear material Guy decontaminated. The liquid waste remains in its underground tanks, the sludge in its pools, and the spent fuel rods are still being guarded against theft by nuclear terrorists. Apparently the government believes that their absence of radioactivity is only temporary. In other words, the government doesn't believe its own official version of events.

And there is this final bit of news. Four days ago federal agents arrested Henri le Strange, who told me the story that I wrote down here. They say his indefinite detention is necessary due to a matter of national security. Marie is hysterical, believing that Henri will be renditioned to some secret prison and never seen again.

Perhaps her fears are unwarranted. Perhaps Henri will be questioned and released. But to me, his arrest proves that the unofficial story is true, and I am in hiding. By the time this is published I'll be living under another name. I'll also be living on a different continent, because I have little faith in the ability of the government to close the lid on the Pandora's Box it opened decades ago.

As for those who choose to remain in North America, I suggest that you offer a short prayer for the health and happiness of a reformed courtesan and an autistic youth, and forgive them their incidental sins. For the time being, they are all that stands between western civilization and the nightmarish consequences of its nuclear folly.

Handsome Harry Blackpoole

The year before my grandfather died, I spent the summer on his estate. He wasn't fond of having grandkids underfoot, but as his first grandson I had a somewhat higher status than the rest of my mother's brood. After lunch we'd sit in the gazebo on the great expanse of back lawn. I'd carry out our glasses of lemonade and he'd shuffle along behind with a plateful of grandma's cookies. We'd eat cookies and drink lemonade while he talked about all the things he'd done in his life.

I was twelve at the time, the summit of boyhood. By his account boyhood had been even better for him. He and his fast friends played hooky, hopped freights to other towns, explored the river on rafts, climbed mountaintops, tipped outhouses, and still got home in time for dinner. As far as he was concerned, summers were hotter then and winters deeper. Mountains were steeper, rivers wilder, and friends were truer.

As far as that last went, I suspected he was correct. Friendships did have a discernibly transient quality in the modern world. I found it reassuring to think they once had more permanence. As for hotter and colder seasons and steeper mountains and wilder rivers, I suspended my disbelief. I was enjoying a special privilege hearing his stories and felt it incumbent on me to keep an open mind.

Sometimes the stories were just anecdotes about practical jokes that he'd pulled on his enemies, or pigtailed girls he'd teased. Other times he'd extol the virtues of his early heroes, Bernarr MacFadden the health nut and Will Rogers the cowboy comic. Occasionally he started stories that petered out with no real ending. I'm afraid the truth is that my grandfather didn't earn high honors in the story-telling department. During that summer, he only told me one honest-to-god story like you'd find in a magazine or in a book. That one story lodged so deep in me that I've kept it to myself for almost fifty years. I'll try to tell it now.

125

I had previously asked my mother how my grandfather came by his great wealth. She answered that during the Depression he bought many properties there on the North Shore of Long Island—including the estate where he now lived—and sold them for ten times as much afterward, when the economy improved. Paper millionaires had liquidated all their holdings and my grandfather had swooped in and bought the real estate for pennies on the dollar. I inquired as to why it was that my grandfather had money when the Crash had wiped out everybody else. Mom supposed that he had kept his money in his mattress instead of in the bank. And how did he get the money originally? From working, she guessed.

But when I asked my grandfather, he told me a very different story.

I heard that story the afternoon a fierce rainstorm stranded us in the gazebo. Thunderclaps shook its wood frame, while zigzagging bolts crisscrossed the charcoal sky. Rain cascaded down from the roiling clouds. The fat drops drummed down on the gazebo roof and poured off the eaves in hissing grey curtains that closed us off the rest of the world. My grandfather paid no heed to this thrilling display of natural forces. He sat in the redwood deck chair, looking inward, with a slack expression on his face. His arms lay feebly on the flat arms of the redwood deck chair, his hands curled around their square ends. In the stark white flashes of lightning, he appeared a parchment man, a powdery skeleton wrapped in blue-skeined skin.

It wasn't his typical reaction to one of my questions, and I wondered if I had broken some unspoken taboo by asking. Then he moved his lips, weakly smacking them together. He seemed to be staring at a spot on the floor. He cleared his throat as if brushing layers of dust off his words.

"I owe my fortune to Harry Blackpoole," my grandfather told me. "The same Harry Blackpoole who ruined my childhood."

These brief and seemingly contradictory statements bewildered me, but I remained silent. It was a while before he said anything more. I think that if I had spoken, the story wouldn't have found its way out of him. It wanted to reveal itself but was so weak after seven decades of confinement that it had to burrow through long-hardened walls of reluctance. However, his voice got stronger and soon he was rolling along like I'd never heard him do before.

"Harry Blackpoole was a conjuror. You know what that is? A conjuror is someone who makes things appear from nowhere. Harry Blackpoole was a magician. He was a conjuring magician. Harry was a ladies' man, too. He had a black waxed moustache and all his teeth and devilry in his eyes. The wives in town called him Handsome Harry when their husbands weren't around. Harry had the women's dress shop on Main Street. Now it's the pool hall. That was Handsome Harry's dress shop for women. Women bought their dresses there because his prices were half what the Sears and Roebuck catalog charged. And Harry himself took women's measurements and helped with the fittings, too. So it was to his dress shop they went whenever they'd saved a few dollars of the housekeeping money. Women in that town bought a lot of dresses. We had the best-dressed women of any town in the state of New York."

With a brittle laugh, he took out a white pocket handkerchief and wiped his pallid lips.

"Harry put on magic shows for us kids on Saturday afternoons in the summer. Put them on in our backyard. Harry was stuck on your great-grandmother. She was a fine-looking woman, that's what Harry said about her. 'That's a fetching mother you got there,' he'd tell me. When she'd come out with the refreshments, he'd start in singing. 'Pretty little Sally/ I wish she was my gally/ Sally O'Malley/ won't you meet me in the alley…' Your great-grandmother got a kick out of that even though she pretended not to. She'd get her feathers up. Warn him not to get fresh, or else. He'd ask, 'or else what?' She'd shake her finger at him and tell him that Pop would fix his wagon proper."

My grandfather poked at the cookies left on the plate until he settled on one that didn't seem any different from the others. He handed it to me and I ate it even though I'd had six already.

"Handsome Harry, he'd laugh and go on singing. He knew Pop was out driving his Fuller Brush route. Your great-grandfather was the first Fuller Brush salesman in all New York. He owned a Model T that he drove on his route. He covered the whole county, traveled six days a week, rain or snow. When Pop pulled in Saturday nights it'd be past dark and I'd be on my way to bed. My mother would start in about how that rascal Handsome Harry got fresh with her again, how he'd declared that she was 'a sight for sore eyes.' About how he'd whispered that he wished her little stem-winder—which meant me—was his own son and would have been if he'd met her one day before Pop did. And she'd lay the back of one hand against her forehead and close her eyes and sigh that Harry made her feel like she was a loose woman, the way he carried on. Then she'd fall into Pop's arms and say how lucky she was to have a loving husband instead of a cad like Harry. Before too long it would get real quiet in the house. So it seemed to me that Pop looked forward to Saturday magic shows and didn't so much mind Harry flirting with my mother. At Christmas, he'd remind her to bake a cake or pie for poor old Harry, who wasn't so fortunate to have a wife to make Christmas treats. My mother would huff at that. She'd say that Handsome Harry could have had about any wife he wanted and that maybe he even did, so it was his own fault he didn't get desserts at the holidays. But she'd bake such a pie or cake that my mouth watered just seeing it. She'd walk it over to Harry's, but she always took me along. 'To protect me,' is how she put it."

The rain had let up. I shifted to the edge of my chair to lean closer.

"Pop wore these eyeglasses with real thick glass. If you put them on, you couldn't see a hand in front of your face. Pop was blind as a bat without them. He wasn't going to fix Harry's wagon over a flirt. Pop was built like a wrestler and he could chew iron and spit nails, but he'd have to take off his eyeglasses for fighting and then he couldn't see where to throw a punch. He wasn't a hard type, anyway. Pop was what you call a glad-hander. You know what I mean when I say glad-hander? A glad-hander is someone who shakes a hand like he's glad to shake it. A glad-hander makes a person want to buy whatever it is he's selling, on account of him making you feel like he's your best friend. Pop was a born glad-hander. He might talk a fellow's ears off, but he would never have boxed them. He never even switched me. I was the only boy in town never got switched."

My grandfather chuckled raspily, as if picturing those other boys getting their behinds switched and weeping themselves to sleep while

128

he cuddled up cozy with an unmarked butt. Rain started up again as hard as before. Again we were cut off from the rest of the world. It was easy for me to imagine a time when my grandfather and his fellow ruffians ran hooting and hollering in their undershirts and patched trousers, pockets bulging with stolen peaches, dashing along shortcuts to the switching yard to hop a freight for Elmira or Savona, where they'd lash boards into a rickety raft that might or might not float them back home. Life was different then. A person had to live like life was precious, because if death came knocking no door kept it out. And death had plenty of diseases in its armory: pneumonia and tuberculosis, whooping cough and scarlet fever, cholera and typhoid fever, lockjaw and rabies, not to mention ordinary flu. Death struck indiscriminately at the wary and the unwary alike.

My grandfather got his throat cleared in between sips of lemonade. He blew his nose on a linen handkerchief that he pulled from his pants pocket.

"Harry had a mansion on Maple Street, along where the old lumber barons built their mansions. You've seen them. Victorian homes with wraparound porches on two sides, bay windows and cupolas, gingerbread trim, sometimes a Widow's Walk up on top. He was rich, that's what I'm saying. Saturday afternoon he'd stroll down to our house. In our backyard we had a stage that we'd hammered together out of soda bottle crates and planks. With a table on it, a fold-up table. Harry would be wearing fancy coattails and black top hat and he'd crack jokes with us while my mother brought a pitcher of lemonade and a plate of cookies. Then Harry'd get up and do magic tricks on the stage. Regular tricks with cards and coins, scarves and flowers. He'd make smoke come out of his ears and fire come from his shoes. He'd make his gold watch turn to black and back to gold again. He'd drink all his glass of lemonade and then hand it to us and it would be full again."

He pantomimed this for me. And then again in case I didn't catch it the first time.

"Didn't matter how often we watched them, we'd never figure them out. We'd ooh and ahh, and clap and stamp our feet, whoop it up like Indians."

My grandfather frowned at me. I felt a tingle of fear on my insides.

"How old are you?"

"Twelve," I said.

He harumphed at my answer.

"Almost thirteen," I added.

"I was only *eleven*," he retorted.

What exactly was his point I didn't try to guess. But the age comparison seemed to mollify him, and he resumed where he had left off.

"Then Harry did his grand finale. He'd whirl himself around and whip off his top hat and set it on the table upside down. He'd lean forward with his fists on either side of the tophat and he'd ask us in a loud whisper if we were up to doing a little conjuring. He'd spout a lot of malarkey about transporting things from the realm of imagination into the realm of materialism. Then he would look this way and that to see if there were any spies in the vicinity. 'All right, let me see your hands!' he'd say. All of us put up our hands and waved then. 'Pick me, Harry! Pick me!' He'd point to one of us. Whatever that kid named, Harry would conjure it up. He concentrated with his eyes tight shut and his body stiff as a board. And slowly Harry would reach down into that top hat. He'd feel around inside it with his head cocked and his eyes looking at the clouds. Then he'd exclaim "Aha!" and he'd pull whatever it was out of the top hat."

"Like what?" I blurted.

"Well, what most of us wanted was some animal or another for a pet. So Harry would conjure a parrot or a puppy or a turtle. It took a whole summer before every kid had a pet, because Harry never did more than one conjure. He said materializing was hard work."

My grandfather brushed cookie crumbs from his lap.

"This kid everybody called Thumper had a turtle. When his second turn came around, he asked Harry to conjure a pocket comb for him. He'd lost his swimming at the river, so Harry conjured up a black rubber comb. That's when it stopped being about pets. From then on we waved our hands to get toy pistols and dolls. But they didn't always turn out right. A boy might want a pocket knife and get it, but it'd be all rusty. A girl might want a pair of dress shoes, but one of them would have a broken strap. Then again, some things showed up brand new."

"Grandpa," I said as tactfully as possible. "You mean that Harry didn't put them inside the hat?"

"He *conjured* them! Isn't that what I said?"

"Oh." I made myself smaller in my deck chair.

"I finally got picked again. I'd been thinking about getting fire-crackers for Fourth of July. But when Harry pointed his finger at me, I remembered my pop's eyeglasses had a cracked lens and knew his birthday was coming. So I asked Harry to conjure up a pair of eye-glasses like my pop wore. Harry was surprised. He asked why and I said, 'the ones he has are broke!' Harry praised me and declared that my fetching mother deserved a good boy such as me."

At this point my grandfather coughed and couldn't go on. At length he dabbed his eyes with his handkerchief.

"Harry scrunched up his face and and screwed his eyes shut and made his body stiff. Finally he let out a 'whew!' like he'd been chopping wood all day and needed a rest. He reached into the hat and he pulled out a pair of eyeglasses. Harry handed them down to me and boomed, 'There you are, lad!' I turned the eyeglasses this way and that and saw the crack across the right lens and said, 'Hey, these *are* my pop's eyeglasses.' Harry blinked a few times. Then his eyes got very wide and he stumbled back. He had horror on his face like I'd never seen before. That was Harry's last magic show. He went back to his mansion and never came out again. The same afternoon, Pop wrecked his Model T and died. He was driving back home when Harry conjured his eyeglasses away. The Model T went off a curve and crashed into a tree. Mom and I got the news that night. The con-jured eyeglasses, I stuck them in Pop's desk. When my mother found them later, everybody figured Pop hadn't been able to find them and tried to drive without them, half-blind as he was."

My grandfather stared out at the rain.

"Harry had this colored girl Ruth who came to do his cleaning. But after that she moved in and did the shopping and errands. There was plenty of whispering about what else he had her doing. As much as I thought about it, she was better than Harry deserved. But I didn't have time to pay it any mind. With Pop gone, I had to quit school to

131

work at Johnson's Paint and Supply. My job was mixing dyes and pigments. It had to be done by eye. I mixed paints twelve hours a day and six days a week."

My grandfather gazed down at his hands and flexed them as if remembering how hard the work had been.

"Ruth came by the house on my eighteenth birthday and said Harry wanted me to visit. I didn't care for the idea, but she promised monetary considerations so I went. Harry had degenerated so much he didn't look like the same man. He was as bald as a baby's butt and his face looked like a road map. He was sort of yellowish all over. Ruth had got him dressed him in his old church suit, but it hung loose like there wasn't any him inside it. He was drunk. Drunk the way a man gets when he's been doing all his life. Ruth got him propped up in a parlor chair and set me up with a whiskey and soda to match his. Harry tried making social talk, but I had no truck with it, so he started in about how terrible he felt what happened to my pop. About how he didn't know that the things we conjured came from the real world and how he'd thought they came from thin air. How we all believed that, not just him. How it wasn't until the eyeglasses got conjured that he knew the truth. Pocket combs, jackknives, dolls—we were stealing them from people. How could we know that, he asked me? In a world as big as ours, what was the chance we'd conjure from someone in our own town? If we'd only known, we would have stopped. Stopped like we did after our conjuring cost Pop his life. Then he got weepy about how terrible a price that was. But it turned out that wasn't the only weight on Harry's heart. It took time for him to get it out, but he finally started bawling and he confessed that he'd been conjuring ever since he was a kid. He'd been conjuring silver dollars and gold pieces anytime he wanted money. That's how he'd lived so high on the hog. 'How many widows did I leave penniless?' he blubbered. 'How many little children starved? How many bankrupt men jumped off bridges so that I could fart through silk?'"

The rainfall had slackened. Thunder distantly rumbled.

"I didn't feel sorry for Harry. Harry deserved the guilt of the damned is how I looked at it. He didn't set out to be wicked, but he liked being rich too much to care how it came about."

My grandfather let the sugary dregs of his lemonade trickle down his throat.

"Then that wreck of a man who used to be Handsome Harry reached under his chair and dragged out a wooden chest about so big. 'I can't give you back your dad, though the Lord knows I wish I could. But I intend to square accounts as best I can.' He motioned for me to open the chest, so I leaned over and lifted the lid. It was filled with precious gems in more colors than you see in a rainbow. He had diamonds, emeralds, rubies, topaz, sapphires..."

"Grandpa..." I said, but he paid me no mind.

"I looked up at Harry and saw he was sniffling and wiping his eyes. 'I conjured them out of the earth itself,' he said. 'See how they're still uncut? I didn't rob anyone. Their provenance is as un-sullied as nature herself. And they're yours, to help get you started in life.'

"Grandpa..." I repeated.

"Harry had it right that he couldn't make up for what he'd done. Pop was dead and no conjuring could bring him back. But you have to take what life offers you and not complain when it takes away. Life had taken away so I took what it had to offer. I lifted that chest on my shoulder and wished Harry Blackpoole a cordial good day and walked out. That's what I did, and you can bet I never regretted it."

I gave him a one-eyed squint.

"Those things can't really happen," I said.

"Maybe they can't now," he said. "But they could then."

"They couldn't *ever*," I insisted.

"Well, they did."

"Can you *prove* it?"

"I shouldn't have to," my grandfather snorted.

My grandfather never spoke another word about Harry Black-poole. He died the following year. In his roll-top desk was discovered a taped-up little cardboard box with my name written on it. In the box, I found a red quartz crystal I could barely wrap my hand around. There wasn't any note with it.

I stashed the stone in a cigar box with other keepsakes. There it stayed for five years, collecting dust with my old marbles, wooden nickels, and arrowheads. In my senior year of high school I got it out to use in an earth science project. That's when I found out it didn't have the refractive index of quartz crystal. It had the refractive index of diamond, and red diamond is the rarest of all precious stones. There were only five as large as mine in the entire world.

When I turned eighteen, my red diamond was auctioned at Sotheby's. I invested the proceeds in beachfront property in California. At forty I was rich enough to retire.

These days I stay in my bungalow on Malibu and write stories for my grandkids. They like my stories to have a bit of magic in them and I'm happy to oblige. I think there's some magic in everyone's life—especially the lives of children, because children believe there's room for magic in a world that seems so wonderfully limitless.

I also think that magic is like a hidden force suddenly freed from the humdrum laws of physics. It can be marvellous, but it can whip about with vengeance and do real damage to the innocent.

Perhaps that was the lesson my grandfather meant to impart to me. Perhaps he was warning me. I think it more likely, however, that a cautionary lesson wasn't what my grandfather had in mind. I think he meant nothing more than to answer the question I asked about the origin of his wealth, and because of my incredulity he left me the red diamond. I'm sure he had a good snigger when he boxed it up for me. He was saying, "See? There *was* magic in the world when I was a kid."

If that was his point, he proved it. And maybe that kind of magic is gone from childhood today. But with the wisdom of years, it's become clear to me that there was real magic in the summer I spent with him. I didn't know it at the time but magic can be like that. You may not realize that it's magic until it's over and gone.

That was his real gift to me, that magical summer of thunderstorms and lemonade and cookies, and not the red stone itself, which glitters garishly in the cleavage of a billionairess dowager in Topeka, Kansas. The last I heard.

* * *

www.ingramcontent.com/pod-product-compliance
Lightning Source LLC
Chambersburg PA
CBHW051846170626
46807CB00003B/1377